Resistance

Janet Graber

Marshall Cavendish
New York
London
Singapore

Marshall Cavendish, 99 White Plains Road, Tarrytown, NY 10591
www.marshallcavendish.us

Library of Congress Cataloging-in-Publication Data
Graber, Janet.
Resistance / Janet Graber.
p. cm.
Summary: In German-occupied Normandy, France, fifteen-year-old Marianne worries that her mother is exposing the family, especially Marianne's deaf younger brother, to great danger by volunteering for more perilous assignments in the resistance movement.
ISBN 0-7614-5214-1
1. World War, 1939-1945—Underground movements—France–Juvenile fiction. 2. France—History—German occupation, 1940-1945—Juvenile fiction. [1. World War, 1939-1945—Underground movements—France–Fiction. 2. France—History–German occupation, 1940-1945–Fiction.] I. Title.
PZ7.G7488Re 2005
[Fic]—dc22
2004020554

The text of this book is set in New Baskerville.
Book design by Anahid Hamparian

Printed in The United States of America
First edition
2 4 6 5 3 1

For my father and mother,
always beloved

—J. G.

Prologue

The year is 1942, and much of the world is at war. The Germans occupy Poland, Norway, Denmark, Holland, Belgium, Luxembourg, and most of France. The Normandy village in which Marianne Labiche lives is located near the coast. Close by is the city of Caen, well known for its maze of roads and railways. The German occupation force is ruthless. Despite great danger, people silently band together in an underground movement to resist the oppression.

Clearly visible in the window of the pharmacie is the signal I must look for each day: a thick, brown medicine bottle, uncorked, resting on its side. Prickly shivers shoot down my spine. M. Bertrand has a message!

Beyond the shop, in the town square, German soldiers are drawn up into two ranks beside the fountain. They appear engrossed in an elaborate drill, so I open the shop door.

A draft of warm air from the potbellied stove and a bittersweet smell of camphor engulf me. Shelves surround the snug room, stacked to the ceiling with dusty bottles and pots full of pills and potions.

"*Bonjour*, Marianne," M. Bertrand greets me, his rusty-red jowls wobbling as he smiles. He's seated on a stool behind the counter. "Today was a good day at school?"

I nod.

"No unwelcome visitors?"

"None." He means German soldiers. They continually interrupt lessons to slap posters on the schoolhouse door, hang portraits of Adolf Hitler on the walls, and drape swastika flags around the classroom.

"Excellent. I have another shipment of peppermint tea for your mother."

Peppermint! Code for Allied airmen! How I despise this web of intrigue and deceit.

"I hope she is prepared to receive more." M. Bertrand takes a small packet from the shelf behind him and places it on the countertop.

The very day we buried Papa, one of the first casualties of the war, Maman sought out the Resistance and volunteered our services. She was determined to sabotage the German occupation in any way she could. The Resistance movement developed quickly into a network of small individual cells, so any betrayal or capture would cause only limited damage. These days we tread carefully. Think before we speak. Trust no one.

"The soldiers are drilling, Marianne?"

"*Oui.*" Jackboots pound on the cobblestones. Will the Germans never get tired of strutting all over town like barnyard cockerels? After two long years of subjugation, there is no sign that the war will ever end.

"Then I shall take time to enjoy a smoke," says M. Bertrand, jamming a battered cigar between his fleshy lips.

He tears a piece of brown wrapping paper from his meager supply and scribbles a message with the stub of a fat lead pencil. Before I can decipher the words, the doorbell clangs and boots scrape on the wooden floor. German boots? A soldier? *Bam! Bam!* My heart thumps like the hind legs of a frantic rabbit. I dare not look around. Hot blood floods my cheeks. There on the countertop lies M. Bertrand's note on the strip of paper. Exposed. Probably proof enough to hang us all.

Resistance

"*Bonjour,* Colonel Bloch."

Ah. It *is* a German. The commandant of our district.

M. Bertrand quickly swings his stout body around the counter to shield the paper from view. "What can I do for you today?"

The colonel says something about a headache. It can't be worse than the throbbing pain in my temples. I clench my hands together and squeeze my eyes tight till all I see are stars and streaks of murky light. I say a little prayer under my breath.

"Don't forget your Maman's tea, Marianne," I hear M. Bertrand say through my haze of fear.

"*Non,*" I whisper.

Before turning around I shove the packet of tea deep into my blazer pocket and manage to read the note lying on the counter.

delivery tonight
one o'clock

The colonel looms above me in the tiny shop, a hulking bear of a man.

"Why, you're a pretty little thing," he says. His eyes rove over my short socks, my pleated blue skirt, my white blouse beneath the blazer. "On your way home from school, by the look of you."

I feel sick. I want to vanish down the rabbit hole, like the English girl in *Alice in Wonderland.*

"Introduce me, *Monsieur,*" he says to M. Bertrand.

My breath snags in my throat.

"Of course, Colonel. One moment." M. Bertrand's pudgy fingers roll the incriminating piece of paper into a hollow tube. He opens the door to the stove and lights the spill in the glowing embers. The paper flares, and he holds it to the stump of his cigar, sucking hard. Fumes of bitter smoke furl about his head.

"She's Madame Labiche's girl," he replies, puffing and spluttering like an old train engine. "A good girl."

"I'm sure she is, *Monsieur*, I'm sure she is." Colonel Bloch winks at me, but his gray eyes are gunmetal cold like the sea in winter. He pulls a cigarette from a silver case. "A light for me, also?"

M. Bertrand holds the flickering flame to the German's cigarette, and the last of the secret message turns to ash. I manage to release my breath, but my throat is raw with the effort.

"Your mother has the dress shop on rue Saint-Gervais, just off the square, does she not, Marianne?" continues the colonel, gazing at me once again and drawing rapidly on his cigarette.

He knows my name. Did M. Bertrand mention my name? I can't remember. They know so much. God help us if they discover that Maman hides British airmen.

"*Oui.*" My voice squeaks. I edge closer to the door.

"I must pay a visit one of these days. Buy a gown for my wife, perhaps."

As I squeeze past the great bulk of him, he snatches a strand of my hair and rubs it between his thumb and forefinger. Tufts of coarse red hair sprout from the back of his meaty hand.

I swallow a scream.

"Like gossamer," he murmurs.

I gape at the colonel in terror. I can't move.

"Take care, young lady, take care," he says, and laughs as he releases me.

Resistance

What does he mean, "Take care"? Is he suspicious? I can't tell.

"Off home, Marianne. No dawdling," he calls after me as I stumble away. The words of the note swirl in my mind: *delivery tonight one o'clock.* I must find Michel and pass on the information. For it is my younger brother, Michel, who will venture into the woods after dark, rendezvous with an anonymous member of the Resistance, and pick up our delivery.

How I wish there were no tea in my pocket, no delivery scheduled, and most of all, no German soldiers marching. Marching through the town. Marching through my head.

★ ★ ★ ★

2

Rain has started to fall. It trickles into the collar of my blazer and stings my bare legs. From the nearby square I hear familiar words punctuating the bone-chilling air.

> *Dumb as an ox,*
> *Face like the pox,*
> *Michel Labiche should be locked in a box.*

The local bully Philippe Fournier and his gang slouch in chairs beneath the red-striped awning of Great-aunt Pauline's café, taunting Michel, over and over.

> *Dumb as an ox,*
> *Face like the—*

"Stop it!" I yell. "Leave him alone!" I race past the rows of soldiers snapping rifles back and forth across their shoulders.

My brother, Michel, tries to sweep the pavement outside Great-aunt Pauline's before the evening customers arrive. His beret perches lopsided on his thick curly hair, and a white apron, wrapped twice around his skinny waist, trails on the ground. Michel's face is stiff and tight with resentment.

"What a moron. What a useless bit of shit." Philippe sticks out a booted foot, and Michel sprawls on the ground. The beret topples into a puddle, and the broom skips across the cobblestones. Philippe's pals, gathered like vultures, squawk with delight.

Can they really be so stupid? Or just cruel, like Colonel Bloch? They know perfectly well Michel can't hear them. Michel is stone-deaf. It happened four years ago when he was ill with scarlet fever. I stayed at the café with Great-aunt Pauline so I wouldn't catch it too. When Dr. Leroux advised Maman and Papa to fetch Father Roulland, I was afraid Michel would die. Then I was kept away from him for so long, I thought he *had* died and no one dared tell me. But mercifully he survived.

The day I went home again, Michel was in the parlor bundled in a blanket by the fire. Out in the kitchen the enamel washbowl slipped from Maman's wet hands into the stone sink with an almighty clang. Michel didn't flinch. Didn't even blink. Just kept on reading. I yelled. Clapped my hands. But Michel heard nothing.

Papa immediately set to work creating a silent language we could all use. Each evening for months and months, we sat around the table forming and reforming our awkward fingers into letters and words, touching and tapping eyes, ears, nose, and mouth, but especially our hearts. It was essential that Michel know how much we loved him. Practice was painfully slow at first, but eventually we became comfortable talking this way. Even the schoolteachers joined us, anxious that Michel should not fall behind in his studies.

These raw memories skitter in my brain as I help Michel to his feet and grab the sodden beret.

"Buffoons!" I yell, a tidal wave of anger in my gut. "Pick on someone your own size!" I retrieve the broom and shake it at them. "Go home!"

The soldiers smirk. How dare Philippe embarrass Michel in front of the Germans. He does it all the time. Never misses an opportunity. How I despise him.

Flushed with success, the boys continue to taunt Michel as they saunter past the shuttered shops bordering the square. The shopkeepers rarely have much to sell beyond the rations allotted us by the government. Except M. Fournier, the butcher, of course. Philippe's father groveled and scraped when the Germans marched into town. He secured a lucrative contract to supply the local troops with meat, and in so doing, secured the contempt of almost everyone in town.

I snap my fingers in front of Michel's face. "Where's Great-aunt Pauline?" She doesn't take any nonsense. She would have made short shrift of Philippe and his pals.

"Collecting cider from Barbot's orchard."

Pauline is elderly now, bothered by aches and pains, and we help her out all we can. Especially Michel. He sweeps. Hauls barrels from the cellar. Washes dishes. Runs errands on the delivery bicycle. Helps serve food when business is brisk.

We flop into damp chairs beneath the café awning. Rain drips from the tasseled fringe, and a solitary sparrow pecks beneath the tables, looking for any crumbs Michel's broom may have missed.

"I'm sorry, Michel," I sign. "They're just ignorant louts."

Resistance

Michel shrugs. "Do you have a message? Am I needed tonight?"

I don't want to tell him. I never do. He's three years younger than me. Only twelve years old. Far too young to be risking his life on such dangerous missions for the Resistance.

"Well?" he signs.

"There's a delivery. Yes."

"What time?"

"One o'clock."

He nods.

"Will you have far to go?" I ask.

"I can't tell you, Marianne." Michel waves my hands away. "You know that."

I do. My country, my village, and even my family are filled with secrets now. I hate the scheming. We must not divulge more than necessary, even to one another. Michel is unaware of how I receive messages, and likewise I am ignorant of the secret locations where Michel makes contact with the nameless Resistance fighters.

"I wish we weren't involved." My fingers flitter nervously. "I'm frightened." I gaze at the soldiers. Their gleaming leather boots clack and clatter on the damp cobblestones. Drizzle shimmers on their round metal helmets, and a dank odor of moist wool wafts from their long gray coats.

"Well, we are involved." Michel shrugs. "Maman says the faster we help the downed airmen back to England, the sooner they'll return and set us free."

I wish for the umpteenth time that she would worry more about Michel's perilous trips into the countryside to fetch these men and less about the possibility the English airmen will rid us of the German occupation.

9

"Let's go home, Marianne," signs Michel, as the soldiers finally form a long, snaking column and head for the château road. "Stop worrying about me. I won't get caught. The stupid Krauts couldn't find me in the woods if I painted arrows on the trees."

"This isn't a game, Michel." My young brother doesn't realize how dangerous our situation is. I wish he *were* right. But somehow I'm not convinced. The Germans are all-powerful. I believe Colonel Bloch and his men are capable of finding anything and anyone they want to.

3

By nightfall the rain has ceased, and a faint salty smell from the English Channel seeps through the window of Maman's workroom, where we wait for Michel to return with the latest delivery. In the distance, anti-aircraft guns mounted on the cliff-tops pound away at Allied aircraft.

We live in an apartment above the dress shop. Before the war, sewing orders flooded in from all over Normandy, but now money and fabric are in short supply, and we survive mainly on Maman's alteration work. Maman takes seams in. She lets seams out. She takes hems up. She lets hems down. She patches and darns and repairs worn-out clothing that can no longer be replaced. Once in a while her income is supplemented by orders from the diocese, mainly for school uniforms, sometimes for church vestments. All these jobs provide a suitable cover for Maman's secret work with the Resistance.

Maman sips peppermint tea, cupping the mug for warmth. "Nice we receive tea with each delivery."

"You almost didn't this time," I complain. "I'm scared, Maman. I don't want to help you anymore."

Maman watches me smooth a precious piece of rich coral-colored satin across the cutting table. She has allowed me to pick apart an ancient ball gown that once belonged to Grand-mère Gruber, and the material shimmers like the setting sun on a summer's evening. I have designed an elegant *robe de chambre*, slightly contoured at the waist, with long, loose sleeves and a mandarin collar.

To distract myself from images of Michel slipping in and out of dusky shadows in the dark woods, I arrange my pattern pieces on the satin and thrust the pins in place with satisfying pops.

"The Germans shot your papa." Maman's voice is cool and clear. "Now they make us obey *their* rules. Do *their* bidding." She runs slender fingers through her hair, catching it at the nape of her neck with a sliver of fabric scooped from the cutting room floor. "We've got to show them they'll never win. Show them for your papa's sake."

"If Colonel Bloch had noticed the message today on Monsieur Bertrand's counter, we'd all be dead now. Not just Papa. What is the point of that? *And* he threatened to come here to the shop. We're not safe anymore."

A short, sharp train whistle shrieks in the night. I jump. And my hand bumps the pot of pins off the edge of the table. They scatter across the floor.

"And *why* involve Michel in these dangerous plots?" I nag for the hundredth time, kneeling to gather up the pins.

"Because he knows the woods, rivers, and marshes like the back of his hand," boasts Maman.

He does. Since he was a tiny boy, Michel has

accompanied Great-aunt Pauline on forays far and wide to gather herbs and plants for her homemade healing potions.

"But he's only a child. A twelve-year-old *deaf* child!"

"He may be deaf, but his eyesight's superb. *And* his sense of direction."

I can't deny this, either. During the dreadful weeks after Papa's death, Michel and I traipsed the countryside together in perfect safety, dodging the German invasion raging all around us. He has an unerring ability to sense danger despite his affliction.

"Michel is essential to the Resistance," Maman drones on.

"Papa wouldn't agree." I sigh bitterly, recalling Papa's letter, written to me just before he left. *Protect your little brother from any peril that may threaten him. He is hotheaded like your dear Maman and particularly vulnerable since his illness. . . .*

"Besides, Michel doesn't complain."

"Oh, Maman." I close my eyes and remember those weeks, deep in the thickets and hedgerows and orchards, when Michel and I consoled each other.

"We can't let the Germans win, Marianne. It's as simple as that."

Maybe to her. Not to me. But I don't argue. It does no good. We've had these squabbles before. Maman is single-minded. She will avenge Papa's death no matter what the cost.

My hands tremble with fear and fury. I clutch them between my knees and put aside all thoughts of cutting out my *robe de chambre* tonight. Maman and I sit at the table together in an angry silence, surrounded by dressmaker mannequins in various states of undress.

Shortly after the clock on the tower of Saint-Gervais Church in the town square strikes one, there is a faint scrape on the back door, no louder than a mouse scratching across the larder floor.

"They made it!" Maman plucks the wooden clothespin from the latch, eases it up, and pulls open the door.

Michel, in his long black coat and a black balaclava covering his head and face, stands before us. I thank God he is safe. Slumped against the doorjamb is a raggedy creature draped in a blanket, his head and face a tangle of matted hair and straggly beard. Together Michel and Maman ease him gently into Maman's sewing chair.

"He's English. Been on the run a long time," slurs Michel. His language gradually deteriorated after he lost his hearing, so he speaks rarely, and only to us, his family. Never at school or the café. Michel is too proud.

"Well done, Michel." Maman bends to kiss his cheek. "Go to bed now."

He smirks in my direction. "Told you not to worry," his fingers bark boldly, before he disappears up the stairs to his attic room beneath the eaves.

Maman turns her attention to the listless man flopped like a rag doll in her chair. "I am Emilie Labiche. You have met my son, Michel. This is my daughter, Marianne. We will hide you here for a while."

His eyes are glazed. Uncomprehending.

"Maman, perhaps he can't speak French." But he does. Very well as it turns out.

"Cigarette?" His voice is hoarse, as if he hasn't used it for a very long time. He licks his dry, cracked lips.

Maman shakes her head. "Sorry. I'll try to get some for you tomorrow."

Resistance

His hands twitch. The fingers are skeletal, and a broad gold ring slips up and down the fourth finger of his left hand. Married. I wonder for a moment about his family in England.

"Can you tell me your name?" Maman probes.

He shrugs off the blanket and struggles with the inside pocket of an unfamiliar-looking and very tattered military jacket. He pulls out an identity card.

"Captain Stephen Crossland," Maman reads. "Royal Artillery, Fiftieth Northumbrian Division." She pauses. "But this is an army card!" Maman's nervous tic throbs at the side of her mouth. "I hide airmen. There haven't been Allied soldiers in France since 1940."

"Stranded since the siege of Calais," the Englishman wheezes.

Maman gasps. "My husband died at Calais." Tears well up in her eyes. "You mean to tell me you've been on the run for two years?"

The man's scrawny chest heaves. "Captured in '40. Escaped. Hid in haystacks. Swamps." He forces out the words between spasms of coughing.

"Don't try to talk anymore." Maman pats his hand. "We'll get you to bed. Marianne, you'll have to help me tonight. He's in no state to shift logs."

"Please. *Non.*" I don't want to go anywhere near this man. He smells like a street urinal, only worse. Much worse. And I hate anything to do with the woodshed. Every time Maman hides a fugitive there, she puts us in terrible danger.

"I can't do it alone." Maman gestures, palms out, feigning helplessness.

What's the use? I push open the back door into our narrow, brick yard behind the house. High walls shield

15

us from our neighbors on either side, and less than ten paces from the house is the woodshed. I strain for sounds of soldiers on patrol, but there is no noise except for the rattle of Captain Crossland's chest as he clings to Maman for support. Reluctantly, I lead the way.

Inside the woodshed, I heave aside a pile of logs, scoop earth away with a shovel, and shift the planks that hide the opening to the underground cell. It's hard work. By the time I lift the last board, my fingers sting and my back aches.

"It's not much of a home, I'm afraid," Maman whispers to the Englishman, "but it will keep you safe till the Resistance comes up with a plan to get you back to England." Better be soon, I think.

She helps him climb down the wooden ladder. I scramble after them into the deep hole in the ground, barely larger than the kitchen pantry beneath the stairs where we store perishables. Always damp, always dark. Maman lights the kerosene lamp and lowers him onto the camp bed.

"Drink this." She pours a tumbler full of golden calvados. "You're in apple country now. The brandy will help you sleep."

The sweet smell of distilled apples fills the tiny room, masking the smell of wet earth and, thankfully, the smell of the emaciated foreigner.

He nods, gulps the toffee-colored liquid, then coughs violently again. He falls back on the cot, spilling some of the precious drink on the floor. Maman covers him with a puffy patchwork quilt I made from workroom scraps.

"Captain," she murmurs, "you will be safe with me."

I pray she's right. How much longer can Maman

keep hiding Allied fighters before the Germans discover what we are doing? Our luck may eventually run out. It is certainly possible.

"There's a bucket in the corner if you need a toilet. I'll see about a bath for you tomorrow," Maman promises.

In half a minute he's asleep, chest clacking, breathing ragged.

We creep up the ladder, replace the planks, pile up the logs, and tiptoe back to the house.

"Odd coincidence this man should survive the seige of Calais," Maman mutters. "The place where your dear papa died." She locks the kitchen door. "And then after so long end up here with us."

I just want to go to bed.

"He's very sick," Maman continues. "Pneumonia, I think."

I'm too tired to care. "It's not our problem, Maman. He won't be here long." I yawn. "The Resistance will move him on in a few days."

★★★★

4

Bonjour, mes enfants. Sorry to be late," our teacher, Henri DuBois, mutters this morning. "I overslept."

The other schoolmasters, poor Papa and M. Marcellin, were killed early in the war. Henri, who was Papa's dearest friend, is exhausted in his attempts to teach our entire senior school. We're all crowded into the only usable classroom left after the bombardments of 1940. I hope he met last night with members of the Resistance to plan an escape route back to England for the captain hidden in our woodshed. I hope we will be rid of Captain Crossland very soon indeed.

Once he is gone I shall tell Maman that Michel and I will have nothing more to do with the Resistance. I don't care what Michel says. Papa is not here to protect him, but I am. And I intend to watch out for him. I close my eyes, and the familiar words of Papa's letter spin and swirl about in my head.

> *My beloved daughter, Remember each time you read this letter it was written in the early hours of the day I left you, and in a time of great stress. Remember I have watched over you and cared for you since the moment of your birth. It is not easy to*

*part with you in this dark hour, far from easy, but
I must. Remember I love you better than anything
in life, and I shall pray daily for your safety.
Protect your little brother from any peril that may
threaten him. He is hotheaded like your dear
Maman and particularly vulnerable since his
illness. Remember you are the elder, and I put my
trust and faith in you. Good night, ma chérie,
until the day I return to my dear family. God is
good and will take care of you.*

YOUR DEVOTED PAPA

Suddenly the classroom door bursts open, and in strides Colonel Bloch. What can he want? I recall his fingers, stained with nicotine, crawling through my hair yesterday, and I shudder.

"Stand, *mes enfants,*" orders Henri.

We obey.

"*Heil Hitler!* " roars the colonel.

"*Heil Hitler,*" we respond.

"Sit." Colonel Bloch begins a slow parade around the room, stopping frequently to study pictures and notices pinned to the walls. Medals clink on his massive chest. Bloodred stripes march down his britches.

He pauses when he reaches my desk, as I knew he would. "So, we meet again, Marianne."

"*Oui,* Colonel." I keep my head down.

"Can I assist you?" Henri asks, attempting to deflect attention away from me. Dear, loyal Henri. So devoted to the Labiche family. These days blue-black shadows bruise his eyes, and his hair is newly streaked with gray.

The colonel sighs. He turns toward the tall, grimy windows, spattered with dead flies and bird droppings. He stares out past the vacant, shell-damaged school buildings to the wooded hillside beyond the village, shrouded in damp morning mist.

There isn't a sound in the classroom except for a soft squeak in his left boot as he continues his slow march up and down the rows of desks.

"You are intelligent children. You want to help the Third Reich keep law and order in this town?"

Silence.

"A boy was seen entering the woods last night. Clearly this boy was breaking curfew."

Dear God. Someone saw Michel. This is precisely what I have feared for so long. A tree branch scratches on the windowpane. I nearly leap out of my chair.

"I think this boy might be here in school."

Absolute silence.

"Perhaps the local Resistance was attempting to hide a fugitive. We can't have that, can we?" On he paces between the desks, hands behind his back, flicking a pair of black leather gloves rapidly back and forth. He stops again, this time behind Michel. My heart hammers so hard I'm sure it will hurtle right out of my chest and land on my desk.

"You, boy, what's your name?"

No response. Naturally. Poor Michel has no way of knowing he is being spoken to.

The colonel grasps the collar of Michel's blazer and hauls him out of his seat to the front of the classroom. "Answer me!" The colonel looms over him. Behind me, Philippe Fournier titters.

"Where were you last night? Speak!"

When Michel fails to respond, the colonel steps in front of him, raises the leather gloves, and slashes Michel across the face.

"Please, please, may I—" begins Henri.

"Keep your mouth shut. The boy's old enough to speak for himself."

Another snicker from the back of the room. *How* I despise Philippe Fournier.

"Perhaps he has something to hide," the colonel continues. The gloves rip across the other cheek. Raw welts erupt on Michel's pale skin, but he doesn't cringe. He stands ramrod straight.

Bloch's cruel, gray eyes glare at each of us in turn. "Suppose you had to guess who might have broken curfew. Who might have sneaked into the woods, who would you choose?"

The silence is thick, heavy, oppressive. Then a chair scrapes on the floor. Philippe is on his feet, hand in the air.

"Your name, boy?"

"Philippe Fournier, sir."

"Your father is Monsieur Fournier, the butcher?"

"Yes, sir."

"A sensible, cooperative man who knows what is good for him."

Rivulets of sweat trickle down my back. Does Philippe know Michel was out last night after curfew? Would he betray him? Why not? After all, his father is a *collaborateur*. Everybody knows it. When people in town refused to relinquish their firearms to the German command, M. Fournier provided a list of homes where weapons were likely to be hidden.

"Well, speak up," Bloch snaps.

"Wasn't him, that's certain." He points at Michel. "He's a dummy. Dull as ditch water."

"Don't waste my time," Bloch warns.

"Lads from yonder village, from Cambremer, they go into the woods at night to set rabbit snares. Expect it's them your officer saw."

"Sit down, you fool."

I can't bear it. "Michel's not dumb," I sob, stumbling across the room between rows of desks. "He's deaf. He can't *hear* your questions."

The colonel's cheeks smolder to a deep chrysanthemum red, exactly matching his close-cropped hair. "Why didn't you say so?"

"Monsieur DuBois tried to tell you." Tears stream down my face.

"Marianne, calm down. Be quiet," Henri warns.

Colonel Bloch removes a handkerchief from his pocket and offers it to me. I'm paralyzed. If I refuse, I insult Bloch. If I accept, I will be accused of fraternizing with the enemy. Henri comes to my rescue. He takes the hankie, wipes my eyes, then lays the soggy mess on his desk. A no-man's-land.

"Sit down, Michel," flash Henri's fingers.

Defiant like Maman, Michel shoves past Bloch, his eyes securely fastened on the ceiling. When the Germans first occupied our village, *everyone* practiced dumb insolence. Whenever we passed a soldier, we'd turn our gaze to the heavens. But when the commandant threatened to shut down the school and send all the children to work in factories in Caen, Father Roulland insisted we cease. *Don't* take chances, I pray, following closely behind Michel, prodding him onto his chair. *Don't* antagonize Bloch.

Now the colonel faces the class. "Anyone with information about Resistance activities or fugitives in this area should come to me."

Why did Bloch single out Michel for interrogation? Does he suspect something? Or is it merely a coincidence? My head throbs with fear.

Resistance

"There is a reward for cooperation," the colonel continues. "A fifty-thousand-franc reward."

Anxious murmurs float around the classroom like bees drawn to honey. So much money. Enough to tempt many a Frenchman to turn informer. I shiver. I know what I would do with such a fortune. With that much money I would take Michel to consult Dr. Berard, a hearing specialist in Paris. Papa was saving for just such a journey. But then war began. And Papa was killed.

The colonel drones on. "Just remember. The punishment for withholding information, for hiding an enemy, is the firing squad. Poof! You and your family gone in a few puffs of smoke."

★★★★

5

All day the colonel's words mingle with the rattle of his boots marching through my head, and I find no comfort when I reach home to discover the Englishman bathed, shaved, dressed in Papa's old teacher suit and sitting in Papa's rocking chair.

"Maman, you *can't* keep him in the house!" I slam my portfolio of design sketches on the dining table. "The colonel came to school today. He picked on Michel. Singled him out. We're in danger!"

"He'll die in the damp cellar," Maman replies. "His chest is very weak."

Indeed, the soldier's chest rumbles with every breath he takes. Dear Lord, suppose Maman is right?

"*Listen* to me! If the Germans find him here we'll all die. The colonel said as much today."

"Marianne, I realize you are frightened," says Maman, spooning watery cabbage soup into the captain's mouth. "But I must keep him alive."

"Why you? Let the Resistance find someone else to hide him!" I shout. "Get rid of him, Maman. Before we're caught."

Captain Crossland knocks away the spoon.

Resistance

"*Madame*, she's correct, I . . ." He clutches his chest and coughs and coughs. Soup spills out onto his chin.

"You are upsetting the poor man, Marianne." Maman's voice is icy. "He is a soldier like your dear papa, and I am going to take care of him."

"Maman, *please* listen to me. The Germans are suspicious. Someone reported seeing a boy go into the woods last night. Obviously that boy was Michel."

Silence. No response. She wipes away the drool. The captain groans.

"Do you hear me, Maman? Your son, Michel, is in danger."

"Where *is* Michel, by the way?"

"Helping Great-aunt Pauline at the café. Don't change the subject. *How* can you put this stranger ahead of Michel and me?" But Maman has no answer. She wouldn't do this if Papa were alive. I know she wouldn't. I swear she is possessed.

I think of the reward. Fifty thousand francs. Serves her right if I tell the colonel where to find Captain Crossland! *That* would get her attention!

"Henri is coming this evening," I mutter, worn out with useless bickering. "For my art lesson." I spit out the words because "lesson" is merely a pretext for passing messages camouflaged in my sketches.

"Good." Maman nods, scooping the last of the soup into the Englishman's mouth. Does she *ever* think of anything but the Resistance?

I toss bowls and spoons on the table for supper and a loaf of gray, tasteless wartime bread. The soldier wheezes and coughs. Suppose he does die? What will we do with his body? I try hard not to think about such things.

Later, I hear Henri's bone-weary tread on the stairs. "Ready, Marianne," he calls, opening the parlor door.

I gesture toward the captain, dozing fitfully beside the fire in my papa's clothing. "To be shot, I suppose you mean."

Henri rubs his tired, bloodshot eyes and glares at Maman. "Emilie, have you gone mad? You know the rules."

"The captain's French is excellent," Maman says. "If he's discovered, I'll say he's my brother."

"For the love of God, woman, you haven't even got a brother."

"But Henri—"

"Get him down into the cellar. From now on he stays there."

"But—"

"No 'buts.' Monsieur Bertrand gave him sulfur. He's got a fighting chance. It's all we can do. And I mean *all*. Is that clear? I refuse to risk the children more than absolutely necessary."

"I suppose you're right," Maman replies.

"I most certainly am. Have you destroyed the evidence? His uniform? Papers?"

"*Oui.*"

"Good." Henri glances at my sketches laid out on the dining table. "You memorized the identity number?" he asks me.

I nod. The Resistance will try to radio Captain Crossland's number to England. Let his family know he is alive.

"I'll help your mother open up the cellar. Then we'll get to work." Henri and Maman carry the gaunt, panting man downstairs, through the workshop, and out to the woodshed.

While I wait for Henri's return, my fingers hover over the pencil sketches I have made. Because fabric is scarce, wartime clothing has become skimpy. Jackets are short and boxy. Skirts skim the knee. I dream of a time in the future when coats will flow free and full, gowns and frocks will flounce and furl. I dream that I will become a designer *extraordinaire* at a famous Paris fashion house. Summer sun will warm the boulevards, which will no longer be filled with haughty German soldiers, marching in their high-topped boots, but with young lovers, arm in arm.

"Wake up, daydreamer." Henri shakes my shoulder.

"I hate being involved in this intrigue. I'm so frightened. I'm sure the colonel suspects Michel."

"I'm frightened, too." Henri takes my hand. And he is. Faint tremors radiate through his fingers. "This is the last time. After Crossland, I will insist your mother stop."

Can he? I love Henri. He loves us. And he means well, but Maman has a mind of her own. I doubt she will take Henri any more seriously than she takes Michel and me. She's *far* too busy outwitting the great German army.

"Let us try to amuse ourselves." Henri sits with a sharpened pencil poised over my first sketch. "We'll practice your English. Then you can talk to the captain."

"Certainly not. I don't intend to have anything to do with him."

"We'll make a game of it anyway, *ma chérie*. Say yes? For my sake?"

"Oh, very well." Anything to please dear Henri. I kiss his careworn cheek.

"*One* is needed," I say in English.

"Of course." Henri deftly draws a number 1 into the seam of my voluminous velvet cloak.

"*For* goodness sake," I continue. Henri chuckles and inserts a number 4 into the bodice darts of the taffeta evening gown.

"I *ate* soup tonight."

"Was it tasty, Marianne?" he asks, twirling an 8 into the belt buckle of a pleated frock.

"*Too, too* tasty. I'm full." I chuckle, beginning to relax a little and enjoy the secret game. I watch Henri weave two number 2's into the buttonholes of a silk blouse.

"Maman *ate* soup as well." Just as Henri adds another number 8 into the gore of a tweed skirt, motorcycles screech to a halt outside on the street below.

Henri's pencil clatters to the floor.

"Where's Maman?" I cry.

"We closed up the woodshed," Henri whispers. "She must be in her workroom."

I pull back the blackout curtain covering the window facing the street, but it's too dark outside to see anything. Boots clang on the cobblestones. Fists pound on the door of the shop. Muffled voices. Footsteps thud on the stairs.

6

Maman enters first. "Colonel Bloch and Sergeant Mueller have come to see us."

She sounds calm, but the telltale tic at the side of her mouth gives her away. Why would the colonel come here tonight unless he suspects we are hiding someone? A sour bile of undigested soup rises in my throat.

"Colonel, this is Henri DuBois, the schoolmaster."

"Yes, *Madame*, we've met. Do you live here?" Bloch barks at Henri.

"Non."

"Surely you are aware of curfew?"

"I give Marianne art lessons." Henri glances at the clock on the mantelpiece. It is already nine o'clock, an hour past time for the streets to be empty. "I'm sorry. I didn't realize it was so late. I . . . we forgot. . . ."

"Stop babbling, man," snaps the colonel. His eyes sweep around our pleasant parlor, stretching the length of the house. The rocking chair by the fireplace. Books piled on the sill of the back window, overlooking the yard. Papa's old upright piano, the oak sideboard, and the dining table beneath the front window. Oh dear. The dining table.

"What's this?" Colonel Bloch pounces on the

large sheet of paper containing my sketches.

The hidden numbers spring off the page. Bold. Obvious. Will the colonel see them? Will they jump out at him and land us all in front of the firing squad? The threat made today in the classroom plays over in my head.

"They are Marianne's sketches. She's worked hard on them," Henri explains.

"Yes, I can see that they are good. *Very* good." He holds the outsized piece of paper under the lamplight and stares intently. "So you're not just a pretty face, Marianne." His granite-cold, gray eyes bore into me. "Maybe I will send these sketches to Germany." He pulls the silver case from his breast pocket and lights a cigarette. He inhales deeply and regards the sketches again. He blows smoke rings and taps ash into the grate. "*Shall* I do that, Marianne?"

He knows. He's guessed. It's all over. Firing squad. Blown away in a few puffs of smoke. Like the plumes of acrid smoke spiraling over my head. I cough.

"Yes, I think I will." Colonel Bloch grinds the stub of his cigarette into the hearth with the heel of his gleaming black boot.

My knees buckle, and I sink into a dining chair beside my designs. Deny, deny, deny. The law of the Resistance. I will deny everything. Even if he tortures me.

"Here, Mueller." The colonel rolls up the paper containing the incriminating numbers and hands it to the sergeant. A crimson tide rises up the sergeant's neck and engulfs his face. I am sure he would rather be anywhere else than in our parlor. Like me!

"Send these sketches to my wife." Colonel Bloch smirks. "She can have them copied."

Resistance

Is he telling the truth? Or will my sketches go to crack decoders who will discover our deception in minutes! I dare not look at Maman and Henri.

"Now, *Madame*, I'd like to look around," the colonel announces.

"Of course," Maman says. "Follow me."

"No. Marianne will show me."

Oh, no. Please don't make me. I don't want to be alone with him, but Maman just nods slightly. I walk stiff-legged past the blushing sergeant. Colonel Bloch nudges me out the parlor door. We climb two floors to the attic, his immense body brushing against the walls of the narrow staircase. His boots drum on the wooden steps.

"Who sleeps here?"

"My brother, Michel."

"Where is he?" The colonel grunts, hunching awkwardly beneath the sloping eaves.

"At Great-aunt Pauline's café. He stays overnight sometimes to help her."

"I see." Bloch gazes at Michel's few possessions arranged on the windowsill. A discarded bird's nest he retrieved last summer's end. Autumn leaves, speckled gold and red and orange, pressed and preserved. Mottled pebbles plucked from the riverbed, buffed and polished. Bloch shrugs and gestures for us to descend the stairs.

"Maman's room," I say.

He opens the wardrobe. Maman's frocks, her powder-blue crepe for best and the yellow gingham for everyday, hang beside her spring jacket.

And below the clothing rests Papa's old briefcase, containing his precious letter to me. How I love to open the bag and breathe Papa's familiar smell. Overflowing inkwells, chalk dust, smudged exercise books. Tears prickle behind my eyes.

The colonel peers under the bed, then rifles through Maman's dresser drawers, tossing skirts and jumpers onto the floor.

"Where do you sleep?" he demands.

I lead the way to my bedroom across the passage.

"This is the back of the building?"

I nod.

Bloch ignores the sheets and sheets of sketches I have tacked to my walls and repeats his search. My wardrobe, narrow iron bedstead, the shelf containing jars of pens, pencils, and charcoals. But when he opens my lingerie drawer, he pauses. Never taking his cold, glassy eyes off me, he peels one ugly finger at a time from his black leather gloves. The thick fingers, bristling with coarse red hair, fondle my petticoats, dangle brassieres in the air, caress my panties, panties I have painstakingly embroidered with scraps of lace and posies of lavender violets. My stomach churns. I shall be sick. I clasp my hands to my mouth and heave.

"Take it easy, little beauty, take it easy," he whispers. "I'm not going to hurt you."

But he is, he is. I know it. I tremble with loathing and disgust. Why would he do something so despicable? It will take all night to stoke the boiler and heat enough water to wash my underwear. But so help me, I will. Every single piece.

"Now the shop. Let's go," he orders, scooping his gloves from the floor.

Down two flights of stairs, past the parlor, into the shop, then the workroom. Maman's silent dress mannequins stand sentinel in the shadows, overseeing shelves of supplies, the sewing machine, and my pattern pieces pinned to the shimmering coral satin on the table.

"Outside?"

My hand rests on the latch. Maman's scissors lie beside my sewing. How I love the satisfying snap when they slice through fabric, but tonight I want to sink them into Bloch's chest. How would that sound?

But I must keep my wits about me. Henri's promise, made earlier this evening, swirls like a spinning top in my head. What exactly had he said? *After Crossland, I will insist your mother stop.* Can he keep this promise? What if Maman makes us go on risking our lives for the Resistance? Why don't I simply get rid of Crossland now? Turn him in to Colonel Bloch. Then Michel and I would be safe.

What am I thinking? He would shoot us all. Of course he would. I raise the peg and open the door. Bloch follows me into the blackness. The moon is shrouded by thick clouds. There are no stars. In the distance a train rumbles through the night.

"You can inspect the woodshed alone," I stutter. "We're infested with wild rats."

"My dear, delectable child, you don't imagine your commandant is afraid of a few rats?"

He drapes his arm heavily around my shoulder, towering over me in the dark. Powerful. Menacing. He smells earthy, like the floor of a dank forest. If I let go of the latch, I'll collapse; my legs are as weak as a newborn lamb's. He lowers his huge head and sucks my neck with thick, fleshy lips.

Boots clump across the workroom floor. "Herr Colonel," the young sergeant calls. "Herr Colonel, you are needed back at the château immediately. *Communiqué* from Berlin."

"Damn." The colonel pinches my shoulder. The ugly fingers jab into my flesh. "Never mind, little beauty. Plenty of time for us to complete unfinished business." I squirm out of Bloch's grasp, but he pushes me back into the house. I am so shaken I can't look at the sergeant.

Upstairs Maman and Henri wait.

"You, schoolmaster, obey the curfew. Otherwise you'll find yourself occupying a cell," booms the colonel. "Madame Labiche, you and your daughter will share a bed from now on. I have decided to billet Mueller with you."

The wretched sergeant. Another scarlet flush rises from his collar and explodes to the top of his head. Maybe he doesn't want to do this? I *almost* feel sorry for him. Almost, but not quite.

"Mueller will be company for you both." Bloch gloats. "It is the duty of the Third Reich to protect a lonely widow. Especially a widow with a pretty daughter."

7

Five days later, at precisely five o'clock in the afternoon, I answer a timid knock on the parlor door. And there stands Sergeant Mueller, come to live in our house on rue Saint-Gervais. It's getting crowded, what with an Englishman in the cellar beneath the floor of the woodshed and a German about to occupy my room upstairs.

I get a better look at him now. He's tall and slender, with thick black hair, startlingly rosy cheeks, and a prominent nose that he hasn't quite grown into yet. And of course, the neat uniform and shiny black boots.

A canvas kit bag, a small black case with a silver clasp, and a large box tied securely with twine rest at the bottom of the stairs.

Mueller clicks his heels and nods stiffly. "Your mother said to come up. She is busy with a customer."

So I must cope alone. He offers his hand. I ignore it.

"Show me the room, please." Mueller's voice is shaky. Uncertain. He's nervous. Good. That makes two of us.

"Up here." I dart lightly up the steep stairs, leaving him to struggle with his belongings.

"I do not want to inconvenience you, *Mademoiselle*," he pants behind me.

"Oh, but you are," I snap, flinging open my bedroom door.

He stumbles past me and slings his kit bag onto my bed. "Excuse me."

He disappears downstairs to collect the little black case and the box, both of which he places with care on the windowsill. "My treasures," he murmurs.

"My room!" But I can no longer lay claim to this room. I start to rip my sketches from the walls.

"Please leave them," begs Sergeant Mueller, thrusting back the hair that flops into his eyes. "Such beautiful work."

He throws open the casement window and gazes over the rooftops. Wood smoke curls from the chimney pots, and rooks argue in the woods beyond. "Such a beautiful country."

"It *was* a beautiful country before Germany invaded and occupied it."

With shoulders slumped he moves back to the bed and picks patiently at the knotted twine around the box.

"Sheet music," he explains. "Jazz, blues, Negro spirituals. Do you like American music?"

"I don't know." I shrug.

Opening up the black case, he begins to put together a long black instrument. "I shall play for you on my *clarinette*."

"Certainly not! *Non.*"

The violent flush spreads over his face. "Please, do not worry, *Mademoiselle*. I will not bother you. Or your family. I will leave early in the morning and eat my meals at garrison headquarters in the château." He surveys the backyard again. "But perhaps I can keep my motorbike in the woodshed at night?"

Resistance

My belly cramps. The colonel *must* suspect us. It would explain why he has sent Sergeant Mueller to live here. To spy on us. It's a distinct possibility, anyway.

"It's full of firewood. *And* rats," I mumble, anxious to get away from this peculiar young man, his clarinet, and his box of music.

"Wait, please, *Mademoiselle*. Or may I call you Marianne?"

I jam my hands on my hips. "I'm not in a position to object, am I?"

"No." A shy smile flickers across his face. "But I have to warn you. Colonel Bloch takes advantage of young girls. You *must* avoid him. Stay out of his way."

Is Mueller insane? I could report him for speaking this way about his superior officer. And staying out of Bloch's way will be easier said than done. I recall Bloch's fingers in my hair, on my underwear, around my shoulders. His fat lips on my neck. My fingers curl around the door handle, squeezing tight. "I must go."

"Another moment. I have something for you." Mueller struggles with the buckles on the kit bag, stiff and new, before pulling out a roll of paper. I recognize it immediately. My sketches! The sketches camouflaging the Englishman's identification. Identification numbers I have conveniently managed to erase from my mind so that Maman can't make me repeat the procedure.

"I was ordered to post these sketches to the wife of the colonel."

"Why didn't you then?"

I don't want them back. I would have to do something with them. Tell Maman. Or Henri. Or destroy them to avoid risking our lives again. And I most certainly don't want Mueller to think I need them.

37

"I sense how important these are to you. How much work you have invested in them," Mueller says.

Can he? Does he realize how much is really at stake? Not just a few sketches, but our very lives. How do I respond to this young man? *Why* is he being so kind? What does he really want?

"The post is unreliable. The colonel will soon forget all about them," Mueller continues.

I don't think he'll forget. He doesn't look like he'd forget anything. Not Colonel Bloch.

"Aren't you taking a big risk? You just told me the colonel is dangerous."

It must be a trap. My head spins. Perhaps Bloch has ordered Mueller to return the sketches to me. Then wait and watch. See what I do with them.

"Send my sketches to Germany," I sneer. "Follow orders. That's what Germans are so good at, isn't it?"

Mueller's face crumples. Why am I saying this? This could get me in worse trouble. What if he does send them? What if someone finds the hidden numbers? What then?

8

The days creep by. My greatest source of comfort is Maman's workroom. I have cut out all of my pattern pieces now. Early this morning before church I have an opportunity to lay the separate shapes on the table, and they fit perfectly into one another like a jigsaw puzzle. Using long, loose stitches, I quickly baste the seams together. The satin between my fingers helps smooth and soothe my cares away.

I drape the glistening coral robe over a mannequin. It falls in sleek, satisfying lines. This evening I will sew the seams on the sewing machine and insert batting into the collar so that it will stand crisp and tight around my neck. Should this *robe de chambre* be closed with buttonholes or simply a sash? I haven't quite decided.

After Sunday mass Maman, Michel, and I settle around a table outside the café with Henri and wait for Great-aunt Pauline to join us.

It is the first warm day of summer. Already the apartment windows above the shops are thrown wide open to catch the brisk breezes. Lace curtains billow out into the square like sails before the wind. Mme. Leclerc waters the geraniums in her window boxes, and Philippe Fournier scrubs away at the bottle-green shutters of his father's shop.

"Emilie, a word of warning." Henri lowers his voice, but I can hear well enough. "Colonel Bloch is a danger around young girls."

That's what Sergeant Mueller said. And I believe it. I don't need to be told. I shiver despite the heat of the sun. "Someone walking on your grave" Grand-mère Gruber would have said.

"I have heard the rumors," Maman replies.

"Over in Douzlé," Henri continues, "the Duplay family have had to send their Jacqueline off to stay with relatives."

Did they indeed? Does this mean that Jacqueline is "finished business" and I am "unfinished business"? My stomach knots. Across the square a door slams, interrupting my thoughts. M. Fournier, loud-mouthed and bombastic, struts up and down outside his shop, fists jammed on his substantial hips.

"Here comes trouble." Henri pushes back from the table, half rising.

"Don't get involved," Maman begs, grasping his arm. "Don't draw attention. No knowing what Fournier might tell the Germans."

No one liked M. Fournier, even before the war. Even before he became a traitor and betrayed his fellow countrymen.

Henri shakes his head in despair. "I hate to see him browbeat that boy."

The blue-gray pigeons in the clock tower of Saint-Gervais flap and fidget. Their tiny heads bob like miniature marionettes.

M. Fournier grabs Philippe's arm. "You stupid oaf. If I've told you once, I've told you a hundred times—"

But Philippe shakes free and hurls the bucket

across the pavement, splashing water all over M. Fournier's polished Sunday shoes.

"How dare you. You're thick as a plank, you stupid fool—"

The pigeons whirl into the sky. Philippe whirls too. He snatches two reed baskets hanging from a hook outside the shop and lumbers across the square.

"I'm not done with you yet. Get back here, you stupid—"

But Philippe heads away from town. Away from the *boucherie*. Away from the ruffian Fournier.

"Blustering bully," says Maman.

"Like father, like son," I add.

"Perhaps not," says Henri. "I'm not so sure."

M. Fournier kicks the bucket across the cobblestones and then disappears into the shop. The square settles into Sunday quiet again, until Mme. Leclerc drags a rug out onto the cobblestones and attacks it with a carpet beater. Clouds of dust drift into the sky.

"How are you managing?" asks Henri, unwinding the awning to shade the metal tables from the sun. "The sergeant has been in the house three weeks now."

"He wanted to store his bike in the woodshed," I answer. "I told him it was too full of wood. And rats!"

"He's not a fool. We must get the 'wood' moved," Henri mutters. "One slip, and the German will realize what is going on."

"I don't make slips," snaps Maman.

"Oh, Emilie, be reasonable. The 'wood' is not safe with Mueller around. We were lucky to escape exposure the night Bloch searched your house." Henri sighs. "Besides, the 'wood' has been stacked in one place too long. This is when mistakes can happen. When we grow careless."

"I insist that Stephen stay with me," cries Maman. "I refuse to move him until there is a plan in place to get him back to England."

Why is Maman so concerned with this particular Englishman? Is it because he is a soldier? Is it because he survived in the place where Papa died? Or does he simply remind her of Papa? Regardless, Captain Crossland should be moved on quickly. Every day that he is hidden in our cellar, we risk discovery and death.

9

At last, Great-aunt Pauline limps out of the café with bowls and a large pot of *café au lait*. She pours coffee for each of us, then eases gingerly into a chair.

"Arthritis acting up," she says. "Michel, indulge your old auntie and fetch the tray for me."

"You work too hard, Pauline." Maman blows across the surface of her bowl and sips. "Paulie! This is *real* coffee!"

"Never look a gift horse in the mouth," she says with a chuckle. "That swine Bloch gave me a pound of the stuff. He said he'd encountered my nephew at school and hadn't realized he was the village idiot."

"How dare he!" I storm. "I told him Michel was deaf. Not stupid."

"Hush child," murmurs Great-aunt Pauline. "It serves us well that Bloch regards Michel as a fool. Less likely to suspect Michel's real talents." Great-aunt Pauline claps her hands in glee.

Michel, oblivious to our conversation, weaves between the tables with a tray of plates, cutlery, five fat, flaky *croissants*, and a dish of golden butter, sparkling with droplets of crystal-clear water.

"Butter!" I exclaim. "We haven't tasted butter for years."

Great-aunt Pauline winks. "Bloch also gave me permission to visit Perrichon's farm to collect provisions for the château. The agreement was I keep twenty percent of the produce, provided I prepare meals for the glorious Third Reich." She dissolves into laughter. "I never was very good at sums." Cunning lady, our Great-aunt Pauline.

Croissant! My mouth waters. "Where did these come from, Great-aunt Pauline?"

She shakes a bony, misshapen finger under my nose. "Ask no questions, hear no lies!"

We cluster around the table to savor this rare treat. I pull apart a roll and gasp. Slipped between the layers of flaky pastry is a round Communion wafer! I trust God is firmly on our side! Papa believed he was. I can just decipher four faint words written on the Host: *Via Dieppe August 19.*

My heart leaps. Captain Crossland is to be moved through the big fishing port up the coast. No more risk. No more danger. And best of all, Maman can no longer object to his removal. There is a plan at last.

I spread a dollop of thick, yellow butter all over my croissant, smothering the wafer, and put it in my mouth. Mmm, it tastes delicious. I lick my fingers one by one, savoring the sweet Normandy butter.

Then Michel brings us all crashing down to earth. "How do we get Captain Crossland up the coast to Dieppe?" His sticky fingers whip around the table.

"Perhaps we can turn this whole situation to our advantage," says Maman.

"What situation is that?" whispers Great-aunt Pauline.

Resistance

"Having Sergeant Mueller living right in our house," Maman replies.

"Use Michel's signs," Henri begs, massaging his temples. "Heed the open windows."

Familiar sounds drift from the apartments. Knives chop, spoons stir, pots and pans rattle on the stoves, as preparations begin for Sunday *déjeuner*. Ordinary Sunday morning noises. But we must trust no one. No one at all. At this very moment, eyes and ears may be waiting for us to make a fatal slip.

"Let me explain." Maman hurls words into the air with her hands. "If we disguise Stephen in a German uniform, he can simply walk out of the house, board the milk train to Caen, pick up the express, and be in Dieppe before you know it."

"And just how do you propose to dress him as a German? March up to the château and borrow a uniform?" Henri snorts, hands violent with anger. The shadows beneath his eyes deepen.

Maman works her way through the maze of this newest challenge. "Mueller has hung a spare uniform in Marianne's wardrobe. I checked."

"Go on," signs Henri.

"When he's away during the day, I can copy it," Maman continues. "Sew it downstairs. Right under his nose!"

"What about fabric?" Henri's fingers dart. A man of reason.

"Check our sources in Paris. Tailors are making a fortune sewing German uniforms." Nothing slows Maman down. She has an answer for everything. "It's worth a try."

"Emilie, he'll still need papers. Travel documents."

Henri again.

But Maman has it all worked out. "Marianne can keep Mueller occupied. Invite him to play chess or—"

"*Non*, Maman, *non*. I won't."

"Let me finish. While he's in the parlor with Marianne, we'll borrow his identity papers. Photograph them. Michel can deliver them to the Resistance. Mueller will be none the wiser. With the photographs, the Resistance can make forgeries."

This is too much. Exposing Michel and me to even more danger. I'm petrified. I tug on Michel's apron. "Say something, please?" I plead, mouthing clearly. But he ignores me. Just heaps our dirty dishes onto the tray and heads for Great-aunt Pauline's kitchen.

Henri slams his hands hard on the table. "The danger is too great," he signs. "We've done our part. I want to move the Englishman to another safe house. Let someone else take responsibility for getting him to Dieppe." His fingers fly with stunning speed.

"I agree with Henri," Great-aunt Pauline chimes in. "We've risked the children's lives enough."

I study Maman's fiery cheeks, her stubborn jaw. I doubt she will forget her idea. She seems perfectly willing to place us all in even greater peril for the sake of this English army captain. As if she were caught in a spell.

10

We sit in exhausted silence until Michel reappears, wheeling the delivery bike. A *baguette* of bread and a jug of cider stick out of the basket. "Let's go on a picnic," he signs to me.

Thank you, God. Another minute spent listening to Maman's ridiculous schemes and I will go completely mad.

"Be careful. No loose gossip. Trust no one," says Henri, ever cautious.

How I hate this war. Before the Germans came, everyone in town mingled freely. We knew the rhythm and pulse of one another's lives. But Hitler has triumphed. Now neighbor is pitted against neighbor. Family against family. Even mother against daughter.

"Stay off the roads. Take the path through the meadow," adds Henri.

"Wait just a few moments." Great-aunt Pauline hobbles into the café and soon returns with a block of Neufchâtel cheese and a whole roast chicken wrapped in a snow-white *serviette*. "It was Bloch's dinner," she chortles, "but what the eye doesn't see, the heart won't grieve over!"

She piles the extra food into the bicycle basket. "No

more talk of war today, or of documents, or train trips *or* German uniforms, nothing," she whispers, planting a dry, feathery kiss on my cheek. A nutty smell of coffee clings to the black shawl around her shoulders. "Not today," she continues. "On such a glorious, God-given Sunday morning as this—I forbid it!"

Moments later I squeeze onto the broad leather seat of Michel's delivery bicycle. We wobble out of the square, with me gripping his back, and gather speed down the alley behind the café, picking up the old cart track leading to the river Dives.

Michel peddles fast over the ruts, and I cling to him for dear life, with my legs stuck out for balance. Splashes of red poppies dot the fields. Pebbles ping my bare legs. When I think I can hold on no longer, Michel careens through Perrichon's cow pasture and skids to a halt. After I jump off, he leans the bike in the shade against the trunk of a gnarled apple tree, and we collapse, breathless, on the thick velvet moss beneath.

"Why didn't you object to Maman's latest plan?" I sign.

"What's the point?"

"Don't you *want* to stop all this? The constant danger Maman places us in?"

"*Non.*"

"But you *must.* The Germans will catch you one day."

"No they won't. Why should they? I get the better of Bloch every time. How many Allies have I guided through the woods? Delivered safely home? Me, the village idiot, deceiving the mighty German war machine!"

I remember Bloch's vague threat about seeing to "unfinished business." Did Michel really deceive Bloch the last time, when he brought Captain Crossland into our lives? Might not Bloch actually intend to return and search the woodshed? Before Captain Crossland is moved? Or even worse, might *I* be his "unfinished business"?

I pull Michel closer to me. "We have to talk," I beg.

"Funny joke!" he signs.

"Michel, we *do* talk." My eyes sting with unshed tears. "Remember? Just the two of us. Right there." I point to the bank of thick hawthorn bushes bordering the meadow, where we had hidden ourselves away during the summer of 1940. "Remember, Michel, how we talked and talked and talked after Papa died?" Tears roll now. "Remember how grateful we were that Papa had created a language for us? Papa asked me to protect you, Michel. I'm trying, but Maman won't listen."

"*You're* not listening to *me*. I'll make up my own mind whether I help the Resistance. Papa would be proud of me." Michel's fingers cut through the air like a knife.

"No he wouldn't. He'd be appalled. Maman has no right to involve either of us. None at all. If she wants to risk her life, that's one thing—"

"Oh stop, Marianne." Michel sighs. "Everyone knows I'm just a 'useless piece of shit.' I won't be good for much after the war when there won't be any more need for a boy whose only talent is dodging enemy patrols in the dark."

"Michel, that's absolute nonsense. I'm taking you to Doctor Berard in Paris as soon as the war is over."

"Ha! You can't seriously believe your fancy Doctor Berard is lolling at his desk just waiting for the British and Americans to push the Germans out of France?" Michel's finger stabs the space between us.

It's hopeless. I'm exhausted. I can't find a way to make Michel understand my concern. "All right, you win," I sign with as much sarcasm as I can muster. "We'll pretend there is no war. You can hear the birds singing, the river rushing, the wind in the trees. Papa's alive—"

Michel's gray eyes gaze at me with such condescension. "For heaven's sake, Marianne. I'm not a *bébé*."

"What you are is a pompous little ass, Michel Labiche."

I knock him flat on his back, and he just misses a giant cowpat by a hairsbreadth. I race toward the river, my dress riding high above my knees, but Michel soon pants up behind me. He may be small and skinny, but he's fast. He pounces, and we topple to the water's edge, saved by the root of an ancient willow, a tangle of arms and legs. Breathless, we lean against the twisted trunk, under a cloudless sky.

"*Don't* take risks, Michel," I sign, my fingers urgent. "We *don't* have to go on helping the Resistance. We *can* say no."

11

But Michel has lost interest. He wanders away, upstream, skimming pebbles into the slow-moving river. It's hotter than ever. I lie back against a boulder, sucking on a blade of meadow grass, sweet as honey, and watch M. Perrichon's cows meander across the top field for milking.

Just as my eyelids begin to droop in the sultry air, I hear a slight splash. The river twists and turns for miles through lowland marsh. There isn't a soul in sight. But I definitely hear another splash, close by. I scramble to my feet. In the midst of the tall marsh grasses a boat bobs gently up and down. An empty boat. Water slaps against the hull. Bubbles, masses of bubbles, bounce on the calm surface. Two arms burst out of the water holding aloft a reed basket swarming with eels. Too late I remember Philippe Fournier, earlier today, with eel traps around his neck.

"Surprise, surprise! Fancy meeting you!" Philippe grins at me.

"Wasn't intentional, I can assure you," I mutter.

He heaves the mess of eels into the bottom of the boat and dives again, only to emerge almost immediately with another loaded trap.

"They'll spoil long before you get them home in this heat," I scoff.

"Nah. Got a trick or two up my sleeve." He smirks. "Tricks are all my old man's good for." He tugs handfuls of dock leaves from the riverbank. "Give me a hand, will you?"

"Certainly not." Help Philippe Fournier? The local lout. Local bully. Not likely.

He struggles on by himself until he has enough of the large narrow leaves to cover all the wriggling, squirming eels. "Keeps 'em cool, see."

He drags the empty traps beneath the water again, and minutes later he surfaces, with the same stupid grin on his face.

"I hope you're leaving, now you've set your traps."

"No hurry," he responds, tying his boat to a branch of the weeping willow.

"Don't stay on my account."

But I'm not going to get rid of him so easily. He heaves himself out of the river. His straight black hair is plastered to his head, and water streams from his sodden clothes. Why, out of all the miles and miles of available river, does he choose to set traps here? Then an obvious, terrifying thought occurs to me. He's spying for Bloch. Just like his father. There are spies everywhere. Is Philippe a spy? Trust no one. Talk to no one. Give nothing away.

"You alone, then?"

I shake my head and point to Michel, poised to dive off the old stone bridge. Michel's pale freckled body darts through the water. He splashes in circles, clutches his nose, and plunges to the bottom of the river, for all the world like a hungry marsh hen in search of food.

Resistance

"What does he think he is, a dumb duck?" jeers Philippe.

"For heaven's sake, you—"

But something else attracts Philippe's attention. I follow his gaze across the wide, flat meadowland to the old apple tree where Michel and I left our picnic. My heart sinks. Surrounding the bicycle, tossing the precious food about, are the boys who normally stick to Philippe like leeches.

"No! Stop!" I yell, tearing over the grass. "You can't do that!"

But they can. They are ripping the chicken apart. Bones fly. Grease drips. All that precious food, wasted.

"It isn't funny!" I shout at Philippe. "Make them stop!" He's right behind me, trying to run in his water-logged clothes. The boys smear the soft smelly cheese on the bread and gobble it down. "Make them go away!" I scream. But they are passing the jug of cider now, swilling it like pigs in a trough.

When they catch sight of Philippe and me heading toward them, they collapse with laughter. "Ooh la la! Ooh la la!" they holler, and make loud kissing noises into the air. Then they stand in a line and kick up their legs like the girls in the *Folies Bergere*.

I can't bear it. My cheeks flame. Me and Philippe. It's too horrid to contemplate.

"*Arrêtez vous!*" Philippe yells.

They stop. Just like that. Odd the hold Philippe has over them. Like Hitler with his henchmen, I think, quivering with anger.

"Get out of here!" Philippe threatens, picking up a fallen apple tree branch and waving it in the air. "Go home!" They scatter like a bunch of silly sheep.

Surely Philippe will follow them. But he doesn't. Why, oh why, won't he leave us alone?

Philippe squats beneath the tree. "What's it like, having a *Boche* in the house?" he asks. River water puddles at his feet.

"Why ask me? You should know," I sneer. "Plenty of *Boche* in and out of your house. Doing business with your father." I don't want to talk about Sergeant Mueller. "Please go away." I toss the empty cider bottle into the bicycle basket.

Philippe waves the stick toward Michel in the distance, still bobbing up and down in the water, oblivious to my dilemma. "Does he understand *anything* people say?"

"Of course he does. He's deaf. Not retarded."

"Well, he doesn't ever talk."

"You've never tried to communicate with him. You're so stupid."

Philippe suddenly lurches off the grass, brandishing the stick. "Don't call me stupid."

He's older than me. Sixteen, big and strong, but I'm not afraid. I can see tears shining behind his eyes. "Papa calls me stupid." Philippe's fingers tighten around the stick. His knuckles gleam pearly white. "Hard to credit, isn't it?" He slams the stick against the gnarly old tree trunk. "He's the one who went with the *Boche*. He's the *collaborateur*."

"I know that, Philippe. For heaven's sake. Everybody knows that." I gather up the chicken bones and wrap them in the *serviette*.

"Always it's 'stupid' this, 'stupid' that." Philippe hurls the stick into the hawthorn hedge bordering the meadow.

"I heard him this morning. We all did. But just the same, it's a lame excuse for tormenting Michel. You're pathetic."

Resistance

Philippe finally begins to back away, toward the river.

"Why don't you stop mocking Michel?" I yell after him. "Letting the Germans think he's the village idiot. As far as I'm concerned, you're the idiot."

He leaps into the boat, mindless of the teeming mass of eels, and begins poling slowly toward the village.

"You want to be careful, Marianne Labiche!" he shouts, far away now. "That sharp tongue of yours will get you into trouble one of these days!"

★★★★

12

Tired and hungry, Michel and I trek back to town in silence. Great-aunt Pauline limps out of the café to meet us, her jaw clenched. And it's not arthritis pain. She's afraid.

The square is empty. But pounding boots echo in the narrow cobbled streets all around us.

"What's happened, Great-aunt Pauline?" I ask.

"Bloch's ordered a house-to-house search. The whole village. He's convinced there's a fugitive on the loose."

My stomach pitches right and left, like a boat in a storm.

"Where are the soldiers?" I ask.

"Not far away. I'll keep Michel here with me. You run home and warn Emilie."

I quickly sign this information to Michel, hug him good-bye, and walk fast up rue Saint-Gervais. German commands stab the humid air.

Maman has left the door unlocked for us. She's not in the shop or workroom. I race upstairs. She's nowhere. Dear God, if she's with Captain Crossland, is the cellar exposed?

I dash back downstairs and into the backyard. I

open the woodshed door. Logs are strewn all over. Earth is piled up like a sandcastle at the beach. Worst of all, the ladder leading down to the cellar is clearly visible. The fatal slip Henri talked about just this morning! Maman has lost all reason. She *never* took chances like this before. What has got into her?

I kneel by the gaping entrance and peek down into the shadowy hideaway. I hear Maman's voice. She's reading Dickens' novel, *A Tale of Two Cities*. We are about to be discovered harboring a fugitive, and she is reading a book!

My eyes adjust to the darkness. I blink. And blink again. I can't believe my eyes. It was bad enough that she dressed the Englishman in Papa's teacher suit and sat him by the fire in Papa's rocking chair as if he were Papa, for heaven's sake! But now she is crouched beside the cot, and she is holding his hand.

I am sick with fury. I bang on the top step of the ladder with a piece of firewood. Maman's book slithers to the floor with a gentle swoosh. The captain coughs.

"German search party coming," I snarl.

"Marianne, *ma chérie*—"

"*Fermez la bouche!*" I hurl the insult down the ladder. How satisfying it is to tell Maman to shut up. I'm tempted to leave them to their fate. Truly I am. I hesitate for just a moment, then slide the planks into place.

The blasted boots are in the alley now. I shovel the earth as best I can and manage to cover the planks, but there's no time to replace the piles of firewood. I brush earth and dust from my dress and step into the yard, closing the door behind me, just as Sergeant Mueller opens the gate, accompanied by three soldiers, rifles at the ready.

So I was correct. He's guessed we're hiding the

fugitive. He salutes and clicks his heels. My skin crawls.

"Marianne."

The sleek German holsters smell rich and buttery, like Papa's old leather briefcase stowed safely in Maman's wardrobe.

"I am sorry. We have orders to search the house."

I nod.

"Go inside," he orders the soldiers. "And no damage, understand?"

Their helmets gleam in the soft afternoon light. One of them moves past me to the door of the shed. He listens. Can he hear something? A cough perhaps?

"I will do the outbuilding," Mueller snaps.

Of course he will. And get all the glory for finding the fugitive. I think of Maman and the captain in the ground beneath us. Do they realize the danger? Did Maman understand?

"Go," orders Mueller.

They hesitate.

"*Schnell! Schnell!*"

Reluctantly the soldiers move into the house and begin searching the workroom. Something thuds to the floor. One of Maman's mannequins, no doubt. Clumsy brutes.

"Do you want to sit, Marianne?"

I shake my head.

"You are very pale."

I gulp for air.

Mueller moves closer. I can't look at him. Instead, I concentrate on the silver buttons glinting on his jacket.

"It's just a woodshed," I manage to whisper.

"Marianne, I must open the door. I have to look at everything. You understand?"

Resistance

I nod. I can't talk. Of course he has to open the door.

"Go into the house. The soldiers will not bother you, I promise."

Yes, I want to go into the house. I don't want to be here in the backyard when he hauls Maman and Captain Crossland out of the ground. How could Maman have been so thoughtless? So careless? Damn it, Maman. Why were you holding his hand?

I watch Mueller from the parlor window upstairs. He pushes open the door slowly and steps inside. He's there in the woodshed a very long time.

The soldiers are in the bedrooms now, thrashing through wardrobes and dressers. I cover my ears to block out the cracking noise their boots make on the floors above my head.

What's taking Mueller so long? I suppose he needs time to drag Captain Crossland up the steps. He is still a sick man. Will Mueller be holding his pistol to their heads? Or will he use the rifle that is always slung over his shoulder?

Finally the door opens. Mueller comes out first. How odd. I can hardly bear to look. I wait for Maman and the captain to follow. Mueller glances up at the parlor window. He knows I'm watching. He brushes sawdust from his jacket and straightens his helmet. Then he closes the door.

What is he playing at? Did it not seem odd to him that the logs were scattered? Not neatly stacked? Is it only because I know there is a hideaway that it appears obvious to me? Can our secret still be safe?

Oh, dear God. I grasp the curtains with both hands. Colonel Bloch is striding through the back gate, his colossal size filling up the tiny yard. Mueller swings around. Stands at attention. Click go the heels.

Bloch pulls a cigarette from his silver case and lights it. He and Mueller talk and talk, but try as I might, I cannot make out the words. Bloch leans against the brick wall and points to the woodshed. Mueller throws up his arms, hands palm up, and shakes his head, again and again. Bloch finally tosses the butt of his cigarette onto the ground and grinds it hard with his boot.

Finally, Colonel Bloch, Sergeant Mueller, and the three soldiers leave and start their search all over again next door. I sink to my knees, weak with relief, hardly able to believe our narrow escape. Thank you, God. Thank you.

I trail through the house. In Michel's attic room his precious bird's nest, a marvel of twigs, leaves, and mud, is ground to dust on the floor. I step on a pebble, and it rolls beneath the bed.

Maman's room is a shambles. Clothes strewn all over. Sheets stripped from the bed. Furniture dragged away from the walls. An effort to discover false walls or hidey-holes, I suppose. Papa's old leather briefcase is tossed into a corner. I unbuckle the catch and breathe in the comforting smells. Chalk, ink, tatty textbooks. Papa's letter is safe inside. I unfold it with trembling fingers and read his words again and again and again. *Remember I love you better than anything in life, and I shall pray daily for your safety.* Minutes pass, perhaps hours, before I can bear to drag myself down to Maman's workroom.

Worse yet, worse than my argument today with Michel, worse than the fear that Philippe may be a spy, worse than Maman risking our lives so she can hold the hand of an English soldier, is the scene of malicious destruction before me. The mannequin I draped only this morning with my satin *robe de chambre* has been gutted by bayonets. Raw gashes gape from neck to belly. Stuffing spills out in jagged clumps. My precious robe is shredded. Why? Why do such willful damage? Surely the Germans didn't imagine the fugitive was hiding inside the mannequin!

I crawl about the floor gathering up the strips of frayed cloth until I have retrieved every single piece. Scattered on the table, they shimmer like shards of evening light through the windows of the church of Saint-Gervais. I sink into a chair and rest my cheeks on the tattered coral satin, soft as thistledown.

Eventually, when the house-to-house search is over, I creep outside to rescue Maman, feed the captain, and properly disguise his hideout once more.

But all the time I plot revenge. I will rid us of Captain Crossland. I won't wait for the Resistance to deliver him to Dieppe on August 19. I shall pay Maman back for holding his hand. I shall pay Maman back for the destruction of my satin robe. I shall pay Maman back for bringing us all to the brink of disaster.

★★★★

13

When school closes for summer recess, pupils scatter into the countryside to help harvest crops for the Third Reich. Only those of us with legitimate reasons are permitted to stay in the village.

Philippe Fournier butchers meat for his father behind the *boucherie*; Michel delivers orders and waits tables at the café; I serve customers in the shop while Maman sews.

And unknown to the German occupation, I also attend to the fugitive soldier hidden in the cellar beneath the woodshed. A task I hate. In my mind's eye I can still see Maman's thumb moving like a caress across the back of the Englishman's hand.

Today, shortly after I deliver Crossland's meal, hidden as usual in the empty log basket, Mueller's motorbike tires squeal in the alley behind the house. I peek between the lace curtains of the parlor window and watch him wheel his bike through the back gate and prop it against the woodshed. He pauses, head half-cocked. My hand flies to my mouth. Can he smell the eel pie I delivered to Captain Crossland for his supper? Or perhaps the foul cigarettes the

Resistance

Englishman smokes whenever Maman can get them?

Mueller glances up and lifts his hand to wave, but I let the curtain fall back into place. He unties a box from the carrier behind the seat of his motorbike and heads for the back door.

"Who's outside, Marianne?" Maman calls from the kitchen.

"Mueller," I snap.

I've barely spoken to her since the Germans raided our home. I can't forgive Maman for her selfishness. It is all her fault my cherished piece of sewing is destroyed. Where will I ever find another piece of fabric so exquisite? Grand-mère Gruber's old evening gown was our last remaining treasure. Soon we will be reduced to running up frocks from discarded tablecloths and worn curtains.

"Come and help me, Marianne." Maman rubs her hands together. "Tonight I will invite him to eat with us."

"What on earth for?" She's like Madame Defarge in *A Tale of Two Cities*, who plots never-ending revenge for the death of a loved one.

"Time to make a friend of him. The uniform material from Paris arrived today."

"*What?*" I turn on Maman. "I thought we agreed *not* to get any more involved. We agreed to get the captain moved to another safe house."

"I didn't agree. My plan to copy the uniform is a good plan. It will work."

I grit my teeth. How dare Maman go forging ahead, regardless of how the rest of us feel? Henri didn't think it would work. Great-aunt Pauline certainly didn't. No one else thought it was a good plan. I am determined to rid us of Crossland. And Maman's opportunities to rendezvous with him in the cellar.

"Marianne, *ma chérie*, let me—"

I storm past her into the larder for a glass of milk to calm my frazzled nerves. A very dead rabbit hangs from a ceiling hook. Snapped in a snare, its head flops awkwardly. Beads of dry blood cling to the matted fur. Its bulbous eyes are crazed with fear. I rush headlong for the parlor, but Mueller blocks my way.

"*Bonsoir, Mademoiselle.*" His jacket smells of petrol and axle grease. "I bring a gift for you." The box that was tied on his motorcycle is now wedged under his arm.

"Welcome, Sergeant Mueller," Maman says, following behind me. "Make yourself at home."

"Thank you." He clicks his heels. I shudder.

"Pour our guest a glass of calvados, Marianne," Maman says. "And for me, too, I think."

I slap the drinks on the dining table.

"Your room is satisfactory?" Maman asks, settling herself for a friendly chat.

"Yes, Madame Labiche. Thank you. But my clarinette playing, does it bother you?"

"Not at all."

"Before the war I studied music at the conservatory in Dresden. Also, I played in a dance band."

"You are very good."

"*Danke.*" Mueller blushes and places the box on the hearthrug in front of the fireplace. "For you, Marianne," he says shyly.

"I don't want it." Since the ghastly night he searched the woodshed, when my *robe de chambre* was reduced to shreds, I have managed to avoid him.

"Marianne, don't be rude," says Maman.

"Well, I don't." I glance at the box. If I didn't know better I'd swear it shook slightly.

Resistance

"You may change your mind," coaxes Mueller, sipping on his drink.

There is a faint clawing now, and the box definitely moves. I'm curious. But I can't possibly accept a gift from a German. All at once the box topples on its side. The lid pops off, and out tumbles a tiny white kitten.

"Oh, Maman, look!" I exclaim before I can stop myself.

Mueller scoops up the ball of fluff and holds it out to me. "You need a cat around here. I have heard those wild rats scrabbling in the woodshed." He smiles.

I am faint. He knows. He *must* know. Why else would he mention rats? I dare not look at Maman.

"He'll grow up to be King of the Ratcatchers. You just wait and see."

I ignore him. I try hard to ignore Ratcatcher, too.

"Thank you, Sergeant Mueller. You're right. The rats are bad this year. Worse than usual," Maman agrees, but her telltale tic quivers slightly.

Mueller bows. What is going on? I can't figure out why he is doing this. Did he realize last week that we have a fugitive in the woodshed? If so, he lied to Colonel Bloch. A *very* dangerous thing to do. Why would he risk such a thing?

"Eat supper with us tonight," Maman invites him. "A thank-you for the Ratcatcher!"

I know what Maman is up to. Softening up the sergeant so she can *borrow* his papers after she has sewn the uniform. But I'll find a way to get rid of Crossland long before she has an opportunity to copy Mueller's clothes, long before she must *borrow* Mueller's papers. You just wait and see, Maman.

"I am honored." Click go the heels. Ugh! I don't

want to eat supper with him. I live here too. Don't I have any say?

"My name is Wilhelm. You will call me Wilhelm?"

"*Non.*" Maman laughs. "We will call you Willi. Won't we, Marianne?"

I won't call him Willi. I won't call him anything. An Englishman in the woodshed. A German in the parlor. It is altogether too much to bear.

"You're in luck, Willi. Philippe Fournier, the butcher's son, trapped a juicy fat rabbit last night. Oh!" She covers her mouth with her hand. "You won't report us, I hope, for accepting poached meat?"

"No, Madame Labiche. I will not report you."

I will not report you. I will not report you. The words slip and slide about in my head. What is he really saying? Did he choose not to report us last Sunday? Is he just waiting to catch us red-handed?

"Marianne, be a good girl. Set the dining table for the three of us. Michel is staying with Pauline tonight."

I will hold my tongue for now, but I'll get the better of Maman yet. I swear I will.

"Willi, help yourself to the calvados," Mama orders, disappearing into the kitchen, leaving me alone with Mueller.

"Would you prefer I wait in my bedroom until supper?" he asks.

"You mean *my* room, don't you?" I reach for the beakers and plates on the sideboard.

"Yes, your room. It was not my idea. You know that."

"But *why* did Colonel Bloch do it? Billet you here? There's more than enough room in the château for the entire battalion." I slam cutlery down on the table.

"True, there is." Mueller nods. "I cannot explain."

Resistance

Can't? Or won't? I slump into Papa's rocking chair. The tiny kitten wiggles off the rug and prances across the wooden floor. He meows pitifully. Mueller gathers the kitten into his hands. "He is hungry."

Despite myself, despite my fear that Mueller has already guessed our secret in the woodshed, I allow him to drop the kitten into my lap.

"I can't keep him," I huff. "We haven't got enough milk."

"I will get you extra milk."

We stare at each other. Giving nothing away. Keeping our secrets.

"Now, I will leave you alone," Mueller mutters with a sad little smile.

And he plods slowly up the stairs to his room. *My* room. Soon Mueller is blowing mournful notes on his clarinet. Soft as silk, the music wails and weeps above my head. I prowl around the parlor clasping Ratcatcher, who burrows into my neck and snores softly.

My fingers hover restlessly above the keys of Papa's piano. What did Papa imagine the morning that he wrote to me? Not that the German army would so easily overrun France. Not that his entire family would be involved with a resistance movement. Certainly not that a German sergeant would be living here in our home.

Mueller starts to sing. *Hope shall forever flame in my heart; No matter how long we must be apart. . . .* The words drift downstairs. I move away from Papa's piano and gaze into the darkened street. Empty now. Curfew hour. *For however long I have to live; My heart to you I give. . . .* His voice is clear as a mountain stream. I wrestle the heavy black curtains across the windowpanes, shutting out the night, and then I rattle the poker in the fireplace, but nothing shuts out Mueller's absurd lyrics.

A rich aroma of rabbit stew wafts from the kitchen. Maman is busy preparing supper. She plans to woo Sergeant Mueller so she can sew a German uniform under his nose. Perhaps she plans to woo Captain Crossland, too?

But I will put an end to all of it.

14

Sooner than I imagined possible, I have an opportunity to outwit Maman and rid us of Captain Crossland. It is half-day closing in the town, and few people are on the streets. Maman is at the café helping Great-aunt Pauline launder tablecloths and *serviettes*, and Michel is at Barbot's fetching another barrel of cider. I slip away to the woodshed and open up the cellar.

"Hello, Marianne," Crossland wheezes. "Suppertime already?"

"*Non, non.* But it is a lovely day. How would you like to get out of this hole for a while? Enjoy the sunshine? It'll do you a world of good." I can hardly get my tongue around the words, I'm so nervous.

"Don't tempt me, m'dear. Henri and your mother have made it perfectly clear I am not to leave this hiding place under any circumstances."

I think quickly. "Monsieur Bertrand, the chemist, says you need sun," I lie. "Must have sun. To help you get better." I've got to get him moving, quickly, before I lose my nerve. "We'll just take a little stroll."

The captain stares intently at me in the dim light of the cellar. "Ah, yes. Now I see. Now I'm beginning to understand."

I babble on. "Soldiers won't suspect you dressed like that." I can hardly bear to look at Papa's teacher suit, shiny with wear and frayed about the cuffs, that Maman has clothed him in. A faint odor of chalk still lingers on the faded fabric.

"No, I suppose they won't," Captain Crossland says. "All they will see is a French schoolteacher."

"That's right." My stomach heaves like an angry sea. But I must rid us of this man before it's too late. And Papa would understand, even if Maman doesn't. Papa would never expose me to such danger.

"Help me up, Marianne. Let's get this show on the road." Crossland tries to stand.

"Come on," I urge. "You can do it." But I'm not sure. He totters to the ladder, and I have to push him up. He's skin and bone, and he reeks of stale tobacco, stale air, stale soup. He leans against the door while I replace the planks, shovel earth, and pile up the logs. Pray God this will be the last time I shall ever have to do this. "Let's go!" I drag him out into the sunshine.

"Ahhh," he cries, holding his hands over his eyes. "So bright. Hurts."

"Wait." An old straw hat of Papa's still hangs on a peg in the shed. I ram it on the captain's head.

"Much better." But he winces beneath the wide brim all the same.

It's only a short walk to the château road. But today is washday, and we must navigate past rows of heavy wet sheets strung across the narrow back alley between the terraced houses. Our going is slow. Crossland is weak. His chest whistles like an old teakettle, and he reels like a drunkard.

We continue on, but he slips in the road, and,

when I put my arms around him, his spine is as knob-
bly as Grand-mère Gruber's old washboard. He shuf-
fles to the verge and collapses into the deep, dusty
ditch. "Let me lie here. Don't seem able to move." He
looks close to fainting.

I rehearse my plan. I will stop the first patrol
that comes by and explain that I stumbled upon
Crossland quite by chance and that I suspect he may
be an Allied officer. And I will ask for the reward. My
plan for that money will surely convince Michel how
serious I am. As soon as it is safe, we will travel to
Paris to visit Dr. Berard and seek treatment for
Michel's deafness.

I don't have to wait long. A familiar screech of
motorbike tires sounds in the distance. I move into
the middle of the road. A fly lands on my arm, and I
swat it away. The bikes appear, two of them. German
helmets sparkle in the haze of heat. I wave my arms
and jump up and down. But they swerve around me.

"*Idiot!*"

"*Dummes Mädchen!*"

How dare they call me stupid. Why don't they
stop? Germans always stop to check documents. They
are obsessed with documents! But the bikes disap-
pear in a cloud of dust, up the winding road to the
château perched on an outcropping of rock.

The sun beats down. Sweat oozes down my back.
I crouch beside Captain Crossland again, but he
heaves onto his elbow and coughs and coughs. Blood
stains a tangle of weeds. Dear Lord, he's coughing up
blood.

"Leave me," he rasps. "Go home. They'll put me
in a POW camp." But I know that they may not. Not

without his uniform and papers to prove his identity. And I realize he's known my intention all along. Shame sweeps over me in waves. I feel sick. What am I doing to this poor man?

"It's for the best," he croaks, patting my hand. "I understand."

A plume of dust whorls upward on the château road. A powerful motor throbs. Louder. And louder. Closer and closer. I crawl out of the culvert. Can I still do it? Carry out my plan to get rid of the Englishman? After all, it's the reason I dragged him out here. The chance I had hoped for.

A car shoots into view. A silver Mercedes. A convertible. Swastika flags fly from the front bumpers. The car slows. The district commandant's automobile. Colonel Bloch! Too late I remember Bloch's whiskered fingers in my hair, on my underclothing, around my shoulders. His wet lips on my skin. I shudder.

But since I feel as low and deceitful as the spy John Barsad in *A Tale of Two Cities,* I will go ahead and explain that I found Crossland wandering around. And I will demand the reward money. In a trance I move toward the vehicle, smoothing my skirt as best I can.

The car stops. Bloch is alone in the backseat. The driver concentrates on the road ahead. He never so much as glances in my direction.

Bloch fidgets with his silver case and selects a cigarette with meticulous care. "My little beauty. What a delightful surprise!" He smiles, but the rock-hard gray eyes are frozen, cold as ice. They creep and crawl over my body, lingering for the longest time on the buttons of my blouse.

"I'm surprised your mother lets you out alone like this." Bloch stares beyond me, searching. Tap, tap, tap dances the tip of the cigarette against the closed silver case.

"She doesn't know . . . I mean I didn't tell . . ." I wipe my sweating palms on my skirt. One false move, careless word. Philippe Fournier warned me that day at the river. What was it he said exactly? *You want to be careful.* Something like that. *That sharp tongue will get you into trouble.* It doesn't feel very sharp now.

Bloch leans his head against the rich ochre-yellow upholstery and blows circles of smoke into the air. "If only I had time to devote to you today, little beauty." He licks his lips. "But unfortunately we must postpone our rendezvous." Bloch fastens the cruel gray eyes on me once again. "But soon, my dear, very soon we will be together. You can explain a few things to me."

"Colonel Bloch, I . . . I . . ."

"You are flustered, Marianne. I believe you have a secret. Girls like you must learn that there is a price to pay for keeping secrets."

Secrets! My secret plan to be rid of the Englishman. Can he see Captain Crossland in the gully? I doubt it. And it's extremely unlikely Crossland can raise his head. He's too sick.

I try to speak, but my mouth is dry as dust. What am I trying to say? What do I want to say? I don't know anymore.

Colonel Bloch flicks the half-smoked cigarette to the ground. He tilts forward and taps the driver on the shoulder. The car inches forward.

"When I'm ready, my dear, you will pay the piper. Do you know what that means? Pay the piper?"

The car moves faster.

"Au revoir, Marianne. *Au revoir."*

The car speeds up.

He's gone.

At my feet the half-consumed cigarette smolders to a tube of ash, reminding me of a small, gray maggot.

15

I'm in danger. Real danger. Clearly Bloch suspects something. He knows I have a secret. I collapse beside the unconscious Englishman. His breath rasps through lips cracked and spotted with dried blood. Poor man. It's not his fault he ended up with the Labiche family. Not his fault Maman and I cannot agree about anything. Not his fault Michel is deaf. Not his fault Papa was killed.

The sun sinks slowly behind the honey-gold stone château, splotching the sky with vivid orange light, almost exactly the shade of the *robe de chambre*, shredded by German bayonets.

When Michel cycles slowly up the road, weaving from one side to the other, peering into the hedgerows, I stagger out of the ditch, waving frantically. He glides to a halt, staring down at Captain Crossland.

"'Don't take risks, don't take risks,'" he gurgles through tight angry lips. "That's what you said to me." He slams his hands on the handlebars of his bicycle. "How could you *do* this?"

"Please don't be cross with me," I beg. How can I ever explain?

"Maman is *livid* with you," he signs.

I dread confronting Maman, but I know I must. Somehow we drag Captain Crossland out of the ditch and hoist his scraggy frame into the delivery basket. Michel pedals slowly, and I walk beside them, holding Crossland up as best I can. I feel no desire now to betray this poor man, and by some miracle we meet no German patrols. Thank you, God. Thank you for watching over us.

It is dusk when we push open the back gate. Maman waits, her face crimson with fury. Captain Crossland collapses into her arms.

"Oh, dear Lord," she shrieks, "he's freezing cold. You reckless girl! Run to Pauline's quickly. See if she has a tonic. *Anything.*" Maman's voice is shrill with fear.

"He coughed blood," I say.

"Mary, Mother of God, child, just go. Hurry up!"

When I tumble into the café, Great-aunt Pauline is already stirring a stinking brew of leaves in a pan. One of her many potions, no doubt.

"What *is* that?" I gasp, staring into the pot.

"Nettles."

"Nettles? Why? What on earth for?"

"To revive that poor Englishman."

"How do you know what I did?"

"I guessed."

"Are you going to shout at me too?" I'm close to tears.

"No, I'm not. Two wrongs don't make a right."

"But I did it for Michel."

"Did he ask you to?" She stirs away, the wooden spoon rattling against the pot, until the leaves are reduced to a soggy mush.

"*Non.*" I rub my aching temples.

"You risked us all."

Resistance

"But Michel doesn't realize how dangerous his involvement with the Resistance is. It's just like a game to him. I'm so afraid he will make a mistake."

"Listen child, once the captain is moved, your old auntie will make certain Michel stops taking risks."

"Promise?"

"Promise."

I lean against the cool deep sink and blow my nose. My eyes sting with the fumes coming from Great-aunt Pauline's concoction, and the stench is appalling. "What else is in there?"

"*Eau de cologne* and calvados," Great-aunt Pauline replies, straining the foul liquid into a bottle. "Tell Emilie to massage the Englishman's body with this. It'll warm him up in the wink of an eye." She crushes me into her pillowy bosom. "Go on home now, girl. And no more nonsense."

I tear back through the square, deliver the bottle and instructions to Maman, then wait in the yard, exhausted. Michel comes up the ladder first.

"Can't you try to understand?" I manage to sign with shaky fingers. "Crossland knew what I planned to do. He *wanted* to be captured."

"If you'd succeeded, we'd all be lined up in the square now facing a firing squad." Michel's fingers are cross and testy.

Tears well up in my eyes. "But I tried to do it for you and me. To protect us. Henri promised he'd make Maman stop her Resistance activities as soon as we were rid of Crossland. Great-aunt Pauline, too."

"I don't *want* you to protect me. I'm sick of your fussing." Michel stabs the air. "I can take care of myself."

Why is he saying this to me? Why won't he listen?

"Michel, Papa asked me to protect you. Watch over you. Because he knew you were like Maman. Headstrong and stubborn."

"I'll take risks if I want to," Michel retorted.

"See, that's what I mean. Isn't it enough we've lost Papa? We must try to survive now. Obey the Germans' rules. Not deliberately put ourselves in harm's way."

"Like you didn't put us in harm's way today!" Michel jabs. "What would Papa have made of that?"

"But I was trying to end the danger. Make Maman understand."

"For once and for all, I'm *not* going to get caught. The *Boche* are too scared of their own shadows to venture far into the woods. I've told you before."

"But suppose here, in town—"

Michel storms into the house before I can finish signing my sentence.

I'm hollow inside. Full of nothing at all.

Maman shovels earth in the shed, and I go inside to help.

"What in heaven's name possessed you to take Stephen out?" she rants, digging dirt like a madwoman.

"You never listen to me, Maman. If you listened you'd know. You wouldn't have to ask."

"Well, I'm asking now." She throws down the spade and starts to stack logs. I've never seen her so angry. Not even when Papa was killed. I throw a log on the pile.

"What I want is for you to stop helping the Resistance. I want to survive this war. And I want Michel to survive too. Can't you understand that?"

"Don't tell me Michel was involved in this nonsense!" she shouts, hands on her hips.

"No, of course not. He's angry with me too." I begin

to cry. I can't help it. "Do you really believe Papa would place Michel and me in such danger? I don't think so. Not for a minute." I choke on my tears. Strands of hair stick to my cheeks.

"But I still don't understand why you took Stephen up the château road." Maman's face is streaked with sweat and dust.

"I was getting rid of him. *Rid* of him! Don't you see?" I yell. "To make life safe for us. *You* won't do it."

Maman is stunned.

"Well, you won't. You just go merrily along, regardless of what Henri or Great-aunt Pauline say, and *especially* regardless of Michel and me."

"What do you mean, Marianne? Get rid of him?"

"Turn him over to Bloch, of course!" I scream. She *still* won't understand. Damn her. I can't believe it. "I thought I would collect the reward, is that clear enough for you!"

"What?" At last, long last, I have her attention.

"Why not? Fifty thousand francs is enough to take Michel to Paris. To consult Doctor Berard. To see if he can make him hear again." My tears keep flowing.

"Oh, my God." Maman collapses on the floor. "What has become of you?" Her skirt is crusted with sawdust, earth, and cobwebs.

"What has become of *you?* You used to listen to me. But not anymore. You *never* listen now." I hold up my hand, checking off points, finger by finger.

"I don't want to be in the Resistance.

"I want you to stop pretending the soldier in the cellar is my papa.

"I don't want to help you trick Sergeant Mueller.

"I want to survive.

79

"I want Michel to survive.

"*That's* what I want!"

"All right." Maman grasps my hands and pulls me down beside her. "I'm listening now."

"I don't believe you, Maman." I stare at her. The tic at the side of her mouth throbs away. She tugs at the ribbon holding her hair back on the nape of her neck.

"Please promise me one thing. Don't do anything so foolish and risky again."

"Why? Because your precious Stephen might get killed?"

She takes my face in her hands. They stink of soggy nettles, scent, and brandy. She strokes my sodden cheeks and gently loops my hair behind my ears. But we don't speak. We've both run out of words.

16

Days pass, and I try hard to push aside the horror of my humiliating encounter with Colonel Bloch. He confuses me so. Is it my fault there is unfinished business and pipers to be paid? I am too embarrassed to confide in Maman. She still spends every spare moment administering to the English captain, and I fear more and more that she is besotted with him. I must handle the colonel by myself.

Today, when I open up the shop for Maman, two letters have already been delivered. One is an order from Saint-Thérèse Convent. The other is a crisp white envelope, addressed to Mme. Labiche, bearing a Köln postmark. This is odd. We've had no word from Great-uncle Hans, Maman's last remaining relative in Germany, since the war began. Because there is virtually no personal correspondence between Germany and France anymore, it has been impossible to find out if he is still alive.

I do not recognize the handwriting. Who could it be from? I rush to the window and hold it up to the light, but the paper is thick, of excellent quality, and gives me no clues. I rip open the envelope and almost drop it, my hands shake so badly. It is from Frau Bloch.

I peek into the sewing room. Maman's foot pounds furiously on the treadle of her machine, and the needle flies through the folds of black serge. A new cassock for Father Roulland. I won't bother her. I sink into the chair reserved for customers and read the letter addressed to Maman.

> *Dear Mme. Labiche,*
> *Recently my husband, Ernst,*
> *commandant of your district, sent me*
> *some sketches which I understand were*
> *designs made by your daughter. Quite*
> *frankly they are exquisite. I have not seen*
> *better at a couturier anywhere. I am having*
> *the evening gown and cloak copied and made*
> *up here in Köln.*
> *Would Marianne be willing to design some*
> *winter outfits for our twin daughters, Ingrid*
> *and Erika, who I believe are about her age?*
> *I enclose measurements should she be interested,*
> *and I would, of course, compensate her accordingly.*
>
> *Yours most sincerely,*
> *INGEBORG BLOCH*

I crumple the letter in horror and stuff it into my skirt pocket. Design clothing for daughters of that monster Colonel Bloch? I am sick to my stomach. We mustn't give Frau Bloch the satisfaction of a reply. Doesn't she know what a brute her husband is? Terrorizing everyone in Normandy. Making our lives miserable every single day. Ruining young girls. All morning long the stiff creamy paper crackles ominously in my pocket. Shall I show it to Maman? Throw it away? Burn it?

Before I can decide, Maman closes the shop for lunch. Since Sergeant Mueller began providing us with extra milk for Ratcatcher, and Great-aunt Pauline began appropriating butter from the château deliveries, Maman has prepared Great-aunt Pauline's surefire remedy for coughs. Every day she forces Captain Crossland to consume bowl after bowl of boiled milk with dollops of melted butter on top. Great-aunt Pauline swears it will cure him, and Maman wants so much to believe her. She pours the oily brew into a jar, hides it in the log basket, and slips downstairs to the woodshed.

Ratcatcher frisks into the kitchen searching for food. "Time you lived up to your name and fended for yourself," I say, laughing and scooping him into my arms. "You'd better catch a rat soon. Or at least a mouse!"

I mash a piece of leftover mackerel with milk in a saucer and crouch beside him on the floor. He laps daintily. "What do you think I should do with Frau Bloch's letter, little one?" I whisper into Ratcatcher's delicate pink ear. "Is there a way I can turn it to good advantage?"

I try to conjure up an image of Colonel Bloch's twin daughters. Have they inherited his striking red hair? Are they tall like their father? Are they monsters? Or simply teenage girls, like me, trying to survive a war we didn't create.

How would Bloch react, I wonder, if a man old enough to be their father ran his fingers through their hair, played with their underwear, made vague threats about unfinished business and paying the piper? Better still, how would Frau Bloch react? Hah! Good question, and if she's halfway human, I think I can guess the answer.

Ratcatcher washes his face, swiping with tiny paws at his long white whiskers. "*Mon petit chat*, I know what I must do!" Ratcatcher darts into the corner, leaps on the top of the cider barrel, and curls up for a nap.

Back downstairs in the shop the shutters are closed, but I can see well enough at Maman's desk to compose a letter to Frau Bloch. One that will paralyze her husband, should it become necessary.

I look up the word "molest" in the dictionary to make sure I understand it correctly. *To burden, annoy, disturb, or persecute with hostile intent or injurious effect.* Yes, that seems a perfectly clear description of Colonel Bloch's conduct.

> *Dear Frau Bloch,*
>
> *You will only receive this letter if your husband has attempted to harm my daughter, Marianne, again.*
>
> *He is a dangerous man. He accosted her in the pharmacie. And in our home he ransacked her bedroom, defiled her underwear.*
>
> *Yesterday he threatened Marianne with further molestation. I am sorry to write with such distressing information, but, like me, you are a mother and would surely act to protect Ingrid and Erika, war or no war.*
>
> *There are unproven allegations that other young girls in the region have been harmed, but at this time I only report the advances he has made on my daughter.*
>
> EMILIE LABICHE

Resistance

I forge Maman's signature, address the envelope to Frau Bloch in Köln, and press both my letter and the envelope with blotting paper gently, careful not to make smudges. I fold the letter to Frau Bloch twice and seal it into the envelope.

Finally, a note to Great-uncle Hans, Grand-mère Gruber's brother. For my scheme to work he must still be alive and well and living in the same house in Köln. This is a gamble I must take. I see no other way to insure my safety.

> *Dear Uncle Hans,*
>   *Sorry to involve you in danger.*
> *If you receive word from the Resistance*
> *movement, please deliver the enclosed*
> *letter to Frau Bloch immediately.*
>   *Your loving niece,*
>   MARIANNE

I address a large envelope to Great-uncle Hans and enclose my note to him as well as the letter to Frau Bloch.

There is little chance of my package arriving safely through the regular mail service without being opened somewhere between here and Köln by the overzealous Gestapo. M. Bertrand must try to get my letters to Köln for me via the Resistance's underground network.

It is my best hope.

My only hope.

★★★★

17

Shortly after I hatch my plot to foil Colonel Bloch,
Maman insists I again take up the task of delivering the
captain his meals whenever she is busy in the shop. Since
the awful day I tried to get rid of him, I have refused to
go into the cellar; but Maman is adamant, and I deliver
Great-aunt Pauline's remedy to the tiny room beneath
the woodshed floor. I smell sweat, urine, and stale soup.

"Did you bring cigarettes?" Crossland begs.

"*Non.*"

I wonder if there is sufficient air for the captain
to breathe and stay alive. "You shouldn't smoke down
here anyway."

"I know." Captain Crossland is a tall man, and he
hunches on the cot, arms wrapped around his knees, feet
flat on the earthen floor.

"Drink this up. Maman says it's helping." As I place
Pauline's concoction on the table, I notice a faded black-
and-white photograph hardly bigger than a postage
stamp lying beside his book.

"I'm glad you came today," he murmurs. "I want to
talk to you."

Did Maman contrive to get me down here for just

this purpose? So he can tell me exactly how vile I am—and cowardly—for trying to betray him? Well, I don't want to be in this hole a minute longer. I'm not going to listen.

"Please?" Crossland is clearly unwell, his face heavy like a lump of gray putty. I glance again at the creased, worn photograph.

"My family." He coughs, a deep grating in his chest. "Please look."

I squint at the tiny picture in the dim light of the kerosene lamp. A blonde woman sitting on a beach somewhere, her arms around two girls.

"My wife, Marjorie, is a doctor," he says, pointing to the pretty woman. "Josephine is my dreamer." His finger lingers on the older girl. "And Elizabeth." She looks about six, chubby, two long pigtails, the end of one stuck in her mouth. He coughs into a handkerchief. "I want you to understand that I love my wife and daughters more than life itself." The Englishman's voice is hoarse.

"Thank you for telling me," I mutter.

He holds the tiny picture in the palm of his hand for a moment, kisses it, and places it again beside the book.

"I'm sorry, Captain Crossland. Sorry for everything." I hope he understands I'm referring to our afternoon on the château road. I can't bring myself to say it out loud.

"No damage done. I'm still alive." He clears his throat.

Just barely, I think. Tears prick behind my eyelids. "Drink your milk before it's quite cold."

He makes a face. "It tastes disgusting."

"It's to help your cough. Great-aunt Pauline swears it will cure you."

He laughs. "She has quite a store of home remedies,

doesn't she? Tell you what, I'll drink it all up if you keep me company for a while."

I stare up the ladder. I locked the door to the wood-shed on the inside before I came down. Why not stay? I've nothing to do. No material with which to replace my beloved satin robe.

"I miss my daughters." The captain suddenly smiles. His eyes are the most incredible blue, and they twinkle in the lamplight. "You and Josie must be about the same age."

My heart lurches. I can't possibly abandon him now. "Wait, just a minute." I climb up the ladder and pull the trapdoor shut. Shadows flicker on the dank walls.

"Josie believes there is goodness in everyone. She should have lived in the age of chivalry. Knights and such dashing about doing good deeds." He sips the milk. Puddles of yellow butter pool on the surface.

"She wouldn't believe that if she lived in France!" I say bitterly, thinking of Colonel Bloch and the soldiers who abused our belongings and the power the Germans wield over every part of our lives.

"Of course not." The captain touches my hand. "No child should have to live in such terrible, con-stant danger."

"But don't you see, having *you* here makes the danger worse." Suddenly a furious anger boils up inside me. "*That's* why I tried to get rid of you. Turn you over to the Germans." I gulp down a sob. "I even planned to ask for the reward money. To take Michel to Doctor Berard in Paris. He's a special doctor. I want Michel to hear again."

"You poor girl." He stares into the bowl of milk and shakes his head.

Resistance

"I can't really believe I was prepared to do such a thing," I whisper. "I'm not usually reckless." My voice fades. "Quite the opposite."

"I have told your mother how wrong she is to risk your lives this way."

"Huh!" I sniff. "And what was her response?"

"M'dear, she cares deeply for you and Michel."

"That's not what I asked."

Captain Crossland blows a thin skin of milk to the side of the bowl. "Listen to me. When the uniform is finished, I'm leaving. And should the mission fail, I will not return here. I promise. Your mother has already jeopardized far too much for my sake."

She has. I can't argue with that. But I realize that whatever Maman's feelings may be for this man, his loyalties are firmly with his own family in England. I squat awkwardly on the floor beside his cot. Despite what I tried to do, I know I don't want him to die. There's been enough death.

The captain chokes down a few sips of milk. "Emilie has promised me there will be no more men hidden down here after I leave. No more Resistance work."

"I don't believe that. Not for a minute," I gasp. "She hasn't told *me*."

"I insisted she look at my photograph." He holds it up to the light again. "I told your mother I would *never* risk Josephine and Elizabeth's lives under any circumstances. Not for *anyone*. I told her I didn't believe your papa would either, if he were still alive."

He's right, of course. I know he's right. Has Captain Crossland found a way to make Maman see reason?

"Papa wrote me a letter before he went away. He asked me to protect my little brother from any danger that might threaten him." I begin to sob. "But I don't know how to."

"M'dear, I'm so sorry." Tentatively his arm reaches around my shoulders. His arm doesn't feel a bit like Colonel Bloch's. It feels safe and warm. A haven. Not a threat. "Let it out. Let it out." It's as if Papa is with me. Talking to me. I cling to the captain's neck, and in no time his shirt is sodden with tears. He pats my back, light little taps. He smells of boiled cod and tobacco smoke and sour milk, but I don't mind. It's nice to feel safe and secure.

"One more thing. Call me Stephen, like your mother does. Less formal. What do you say?"

I think about it. I probably will.

18

The days roll on. Now I deliver Stephen's meals with pleasure. I read to him whenever I can and pray his ordeal will soon be over—that he will reach Dieppe, then travel safely to England, where his family surely must have given up hope of his survival.

This afternoon, when I check M. Bertrand's window for messages, the brown medicine bottle lies uncorked on its side. I push open the door, familiar pangs of alarm churning in my stomach.

"Your Maman's prescription is ready," calls M. Bertrand from his perch behind the counter. His russet cheeks glow in the dusky light.

"*Oui.*"

"Tell Emilie to use these tonight," says M. Bertrand, popping two white pills into an empty bottle. "They should take care of her problem." He passes the container across the counter. "You understand?"

Oh yes. I understand. I understand only too well. Tonight Maman and Henri will attempt to drug Sergeant Mueller and photograph his military identification papers. One last time Michel will risk his life to deliver the film. Only Maman's promise to cease her involvement with the Resistance after Stephen's departure keeps me going.

When I arrive home, Mueller and Michel are on the parlor floor playing with Ratcatcher. When did Michel get so friendly with Mueller? I hadn't noticed. But I suppose I wouldn't have. I've been avoiding the parlor, spending my time in the workroom. Sketching outfits. Making tissue patterns. Aching for a piece of cloth with which to make my *robe de chambre*. Dreaming of a time when I might be free to follow my heart.

"There you are, Marianne," Maman says with a smile. "Did Monsieur Bertrand fill my prescription?"

"It's on the draining board." I gesture toward the kitchen.

"Good girl," Maman says. "Willi has brought us sausages for supper. Isn't that nice?"

I shrug.

"*And* Willi tells me Colonel Bloch has been called back to Germany."

My heart skips a beat. Now that *is* good news. Perhaps he won't return!

"You shall eat with us, Willi. Share the sausages. I insist. Henri is joining us too. There is more than enough for everyone." Maman hurries off to prepare the meal.

Mueller lifts himself off the hearthrug. "*Guten Tag*, Marianne." His heels click.

I wince. "I wish you wouldn't do that."

"I apologize." Mueller blushes. "Open this, please." He pulls out a brown paper parcel from behind Papa's rocking chair.

I shake my head.

"Marianne, I know what the soldiers did to your

sewing. I wish to make amends."

Michel amuses Ratcatcher with a long rainbow string, made from scraps of leftover fabric. Ratcatcher twirls and somersaults like an acrobat. Michel and I have not spoken of the Resistance since the horrible day he rescued the captain and me on the château road, the day I gambled with all our lives.

"Why don't you just leave us alone, Sergeant Mueller? When you moved in here, you said we'd hardly know you were in the house." I'm in a foul mood, petrified Maman's plan might go awry, petrified for Michel's safety.

"Well, I—"

"You think you can fool us with your good manners and your gifts. A cat. Milk. Sausages. Now this." I grab the parcel and throw it on the floor. "I know what you're up to." I wrench open my satchel and lay a charcoal sketch on the sideboard. The usual cover-up for Henri's visit.

"What am I up to, then?" Mueller asks, considering my work.

"You're spying. Reporting to Colonel Bloch everything we do."

"He is not even here!"

"Pah!"

"Is there a reason I should be? Spying, I mean?" Mueller's cheeks bloom like orchard apples.

"No, of course not." But I've done it again, used that sharp tongue of mine. Philippe warned me. Why can't I keep my mouth shut?

Mueller leans against the sideboard and stares hard at me. "I wish the war to end, just as much as you."

"You'll get into trouble talking like that," I snap. "What if I reported you?"

"Would you?" Mueller tugs at the soft black hair flopping over his forehead.

Would I? Who knows? Why should I trust him?

"What do you think?" I bark.

"I do not know, Marianne." Mueller swallows. His Adam's apple bobs up and down. "You are unlike any girl I have ever known."

I have no response to this. Mueller disturbs me. I dig through my satchel for charcoal and concentrate on the half-completed portrait of Michel.

"Do you have a *beau*?"

"A *what*?"

"A young man?"

"Of course not."

"Why of course not? You are beautiful. The most beautiful girl I have ever seen. Old enough that many young men would wish to court with you."

Why is he speaking to me like this? Michel watches our lips move. How much does he understand? I'm mortified. Why doesn't Sergeant Mueller stop?

"I wish for just a little of the attention you lavish on your art."

"I've no idea what you're talking about."

"If I were French, not German, and there were no war, would you walk out with me?"

"What?"

"Be my girl." His voice is so soft I can barely hear him.

"Your girl!" I can't believe this. Mueller, billeted here against my wishes, probably spying on all of us, asking me to be his girl. "How *dare* you." I bend over my portrait and blow hard. Fine black dust sprays over the sleeve of his jacket. "You're mad." I storm out of the parlor. "Quite mad!"

Resistance

I tear downstairs to the shop and glare at my reflection in the full-length mirror where customers used to preen before the war. Beautiful? What does it mean? I see a disheveled girl with long, wavy yellow hair. Blazing sea-glass-blue eyes in a pale oval face. And I see traces of Papa in the reflection as well, in the tilt of my head and the arch of my eyebrows.

I flounce into Maman's workroom, and Michel appears almost immediately, clutching Mueller's parcel. "He means well," his fingers sign. He thrusts the gift on the worktable. "Open it."

I gaze at the shelves of threads, spools, paper patterns, and a stack of navy-blue serge to make school uniforms. The silent mannequins. The sewing machine threaded with a heavy black cotton. "I can't," I whisper.

Michel peels back the brown paper.

And I gulp for air. My breath snags in my throat. A length of raw silk, shot through with watery shadows, glistens in the dusky light. I rub the fabric between my fingers, stroke my palms against the shining coolness. Spellbound, I fling the material high in the air and watch it flutter down to the table in a golden pool of loops and folds.

★ ★ ★ ★

19

Mueller's sausage is delicious, but I can't swallow more than a mouthful. My stomach is a mass of knots. His jacket hangs over the back of his chair. There is a large damp smudge where he has tried to sponge away the charcoal dust I sprayed on the sleeve.

Mueller insists he isn't spying. Am I wrong about him? Did Mueller give me the silk because he is genuinely sickened by the soldiers' behavior? Because he truly understands my passion for art and design? Not because Bloch ordered him to insinuate his way into our family?

After supper Henri fetches my easel, and Michel poses, still as a statue, beside the back-parlor window. I can barely hold the charcoal steady, I'm so nervous. Michel is about to risk his life again for Stephen's sake. I pray with all my heart that this will be the very last time, that Maman will keep her word.

Maman and Mueller remain at the dining table. Maman has refilled a pitcher from the cider barrel in the kitchen and keeps Mueller's mug filled. Worse, she is entertaining him with family photographs. Snapshots of her parents, Grand-père and Grand-mère Gruber, when they were young sweethearts in Germany, before the Great War, before they settled in Normandy to farm. Does Mueller really need to know my grandparents were German? Now she is showing him pictures of me as a baby!

Why did Mueller suggest I be his girl? Doesn't he know what happens to French girls who consort with Germans? In Caen they are spat on routinely, and Great-aunt Pauline predicts that when the war is over, much worse will occur.

"Excuse me, Madame Labiche, for just a few minutes." Chair legs squeal across the floor. Heels click. Ugh!

When Maman is quite sure he has gone upstairs, she looks at us. "Now?"

"*Oui*," Henri answers. "*Maintenant!*"

Maman drops the pills, collected earlier from the chemist's, into the sergeant's cider. I watch, mesmerized, as they froth, foam, and then dissolve in a matter of seconds. Could they make Mueller very ill? Even die? I push the thought away.

Upstairs the lavatory flushes.

"Are we ready?" Maman asks.

Mueller's unsteady footsteps descend the stairs. Too late now, if we are not. I lick my lips, which are dry as parchment, and take a deep breath.

Mueller returns to the table and gulps the drugged drink. "Madame, you serve the best cider in Normandy," he says, smacking his lips.

A hysterical laugh bubbles in my gut. Oh, Sergeant, if you only knew.

"*Merci.*" Maman smiles, but the telltale tic beats at the side of her mouth. She is nervous. "Willi, sit in the rocking chair. You will be more comfortable."

Mueller staggers over to the fireplace and sits down heavily. "I enjoy your hospitality. So far from home."

Mueller hiccups. "It is lonely for me."

Maman fills his mug yet again "Of course it is," she croons. She plucks my kitten from the sideboard and plops him in Mueller's lap. "Here you are." Ratcatcher dances in a wobbly circle. "Just relax while I wash the supper dishes."

Mueller stares into the grate, absently stroking Ratcatcher's snow-white fur. What will happen? Will the pills work? Yes! With no warning Mueller's head slumps back, and the mug clatters into the hearth. A spray of cider splashes onto the cold gray ashes in the grate. Ratcatcher leaps off Mueller's knees and lands on four stiff legs, hissing. I drop my charcoal, and it snaps in two pieces. Dear God, M. Bertrand's pills have done their job well. Sergeant Mueller's arms hang lifeless over the sides of the rocking chair, and his legs splay across the rug.

"Will he be all right, Henri?" I whisper.

"I hope so, *ma chérie*, I hope so," he replies, removing an ungainly camera from his briefcase.

"Right. Let's start." Maman plucks the military papers from the breast pocket of Mueller's uniform, still hanging over the chair. "How cunning, Marianne, to soil his jacket so he was obliged to remove it."

Not clever at all, Maman. Mueller upset me. I lost my temper. But I don't bother to explain.

Maman spreads the documents flat on the table while Henri tinkers with the camera. Adjusts the lens. *Click, click, click*; it takes only seconds.

"Ready, Michel?" asks Henri, removing the film.

And he is. Already dressed in his baggy black coat and balaclava helmet, he slips the film in his pocket.

"Michel." My sign is pinched, crabbed with fear. "Please be careful. Don't take any chances."

Resistance

He shrugs, optimistic as ever, and disappears silently into the darkness to deliver the pictures to the Resistance. Dear God, keep Michel safe.

Maman reassembles Mueller's papers and returns them to his jacket.

"I hope he won't suspect anything," says Henri, staring at Mueller slumped in the rocking chair. Papa's chair.

"Don't worry, Henri. Everything is going according to plan. The uniform is ready. As soon as we get the forged papers back from the Resistance, Stephen will be ready to go. Believe it or not, Pauline's remedy is doing the trick."

"It's a real blessing they've decided to move him on Calvados Festival Day," Henri whispers. "With Bloch out of the way, the Germans will be less vigilant. They'll be more interested in tasting all our brandies than in looking for a British officer masquerading as a German sergeant."

Maman helps Henri stow the camera back into his briefcase with trembling hands, but she doesn't speak. Perhaps she is imaging our empty cellar after Stephen has returned to his wife and family in England.

"Emilie, see me down to the street," says Henri. "And lock up behind me."

"What if Mueller wakes up?" I ask.

Maman shakes her head. "He'll be unconscious for hours."

★ ★ ★ ★

20

Before I even finish packing up my charcoals, Mueller groans. His legs twitch. Good Lord. Don't wake up. Please don't.

"My head. It hurts," he moans.

If I keep absolutely quiet, perhaps he'll pass out again. I crouch, quiet as a mouse. But his eyes are open now.

"I feel awful." He tries to sit up. "Marianne?"

"It's your own fault. You drank too much."

"Where is your mother?" He peers around the room but isn't focusing very well. "Michel? Henri?"

"Henri had to leave before curfew." The truth. "Michel and Maman went to bed." A lie.

I pray Mueller is too drunk to start snooping around.

"So silly." His voice is thick and slurred.

"What is?"

"If there were no war, we would all be friends. Is it not true? Say it is."

He's probably right. But I won't give him the satisfaction of saying so.

"There *is* a war."

Resistance

I wrap Michel's portrait in a piece of linen and slide it into my satchel.

"I am trapped." He gazes at me with bloodshot eyes.

"Trapped?"

"In the army. Everyone my age must fight. . . ." The words are difficult to follow, all mixed up together. "But I do not wish to kill anyone." He burps, then blushes with embarrassment. I snatch Ratcatcher from the top of Papa's piano, where he has taken refuge, and bury my face in his warm fur.

"Marianne, if things were different—"

"Don't start that again." I sink, exhausted, onto the rug, cuddling Ratcatcher. I don't want to think about being Mueller's girl. Anyone's girl. Anyway, as far as I know, he is a spy just trying to string me along.

"Ach, it hurts," he wails, clutching his head. He looks pathetic.

"How old are you anyway?" I can't resist asking.

"Twenty-two."

"I don't know a thing about you. Except you play the clarinet. And like American jazz."

"I know plenty about you. And Michel. And your mother."

Does he? Does he know that right now Michel is out somewhere in the countryside handing over the film to be processed into papers for Captain Crossland? Does he know that Maman is probably in the hideaway right now holding the Englishman's hand?

Mueller slumps forward in the rocking chair, close to my face. His eyes are glassy. If he tries to kiss me, I swear I'll kill him. My heart hammers against my ribs. He reaches for me, and I slide my arm across the hearth. Now his hand hovers on my neck. My fingers fasten around the iron poker. He touches my shoulder. I raise the poker high above his head. But he's quicker. He draws a long stray hair from the collar of my blouse.

"*What* do you think you're doing?"

The poker clatters into the hearth, and Ratcatcher leaps again, hissing in fury. Mueller dangles the single hair in the air between us. "May I keep it?"

Suddenly I want to laugh. "Keep it? What on earth for?"

"A keepsake."

"Don't be ridiculous."

"Something to remind me of you. Wherever I am. Wherever I go."

With enormous difficulty he heaves out of the rocker and staggers over to his jacket, hanging on the back of the dining chair. My heart hurtles halfway into my throat. Will he realize we've handled his papers? But he pulls a small, red, leather-bound book from the pocket, opens it, and lays the single strand of hair between the pages. "My diary." He blinks.

Prickles of doubt stab at the skin of my arms and legs. Is he telling me the truth? Or is all this foolishness just a way to make me trust him?

He grips the back of the chair. "This damned war! It is stupid. Hitler is mad." He waves one arm in the air. "Hundreds of thousands of people dying. For what?"

I just shake my head, yes. What can I say? He's right.

"Can I tell you something I have not dared to tell a living soul? I am afraid. Scared out of my wits." His voice is soft and slurred with cider and sleeping pills. I can barely hear him. "And another thing. I love you. From the first moment I saw you here in this room, I have loved you."

Resistance

I wish he'd stop. I don't want him to love me. I don't. I don't.

Mueller holds out his hand. I look at it. Really look. The fingers are long and slender, with perfectly sculpted, shell-shaped nails. How I would delight in drawing this hand. I allow him to pull me to my feet. I am almost as tall as the sergeant. We stand close to each other. "Please do not laugh at me." The sergeant gulps. A slow burning flush covers his face. "I could not bear it if you laughed."

I can't speak. My mouth is bone dry. But I shake my head. I will not laugh.

He rests his hands on my shoulders. "Marianne, please, please—"

Maman's feet sound on the stairs. Thank you, God. She can deal with the drugged, lovesick sergeant.

"Good night," I manage to whisper.

And I stumble upstairs, snagging my skirt on the banister. My eyes blur with tears. Damn him. I don't know why I'm crying. I don't even like him. Of course I don't.

★★★★

21

Safe in the room I share with Maman, I can't stop crying. I'm shaking from head to foot. Did Mueller intend to kiss me? I think he did. I can still feel his hands trembling on my shoulders, his breath on my cheek, and the thud of his heart against his ribs.

The church clock strikes midnight.

Somewhere out in the darkness Michel is delivering the film. Please God, keep him safe. I drag Papa's old briefcase from the wardrobe and take out his letter. I fall in a heap on the bed, holding the sheet of paper close to my heart, waiting for the sound of Michel's footsteps.

The clock strikes one. Then two. Maman does not come to bed. Guns on the shore grumble away. A patrol marches by on the cobblestones outside. An owl hoots. The clock strikes three.

When I finally hear Michel's soft tread moving past the door, up to his attic room, relief sweeps over me like a fresh spring rain. He has returned. His last mission accomplished. I stagger up from the bed, slip Papa's letter back into its hiding place, and fall into a restless, fitful sleep.

I wake to the sound of the sewing machine clanking

Resistance

faintly below me in the workroom. *Clickety-clack, clickety-clack.* Maman, hard at work already. Is she concerned for us at all? Michel might so easily have been seized by a German patrol. Sergeant Mueller might have realized we tricked him. But I need no reminders of the sergeant and his foolish declarations. I wait for the sound of his motorbike tires squealing down the alley before I get up to prepare Stephen's breakfast.

I boil the milk as usual, add a glob of butter, slice a plate of sausage left from last evening's supper, and pack it all into the log basket.

"Come on, Ratcatcher. Let's go visiting."

He needs no second invitation. The smell of Great-aunt Pauline's concoction is invitation enough. He prances through the backyard behind me. I lock the woodshed door on the inside, clear away the earth and logs, and climb down the ladder into the cellar. Stephen lies on his cot, trying to read by the light of the kerosene lamp, but it is becoming increasingly difficult for him. His eyes are very strained after weeks of living in darkness.

"Good morning, m'dear."

I place his breakfast on the table by his bed.

"Michel is safe?" Stephen's blue eyes flicker with anxiety.

"*Oui.*" At long last, Michel is safe. Maman will surely keep her promise now. No more Allies hidden here in the cellar. No more involvement in the Resistance movement.

"And he delivered the film?"

I nod. "But don't ask me where he went. Or who he met."

"I won't." Stephen sips the milk.

"I know no one beyond our own small group. If I'm caught, I can't incriminate too many people." Bloch's

105

threat of a firing squad looms in my mind. *Poof! You and your family gone in a few puffs of smoke.*

"Better times ahead, m'dear." Stephen smiles. "Your mother has finished the uniform. As soon as the papers are forged, I'll be gone. Then you and Emilie and Michel will be secure."

Secure? Images of Colonel Bloch's stony, lifeless eyes, the repulsive whiskered fingers, the threats of unfinished business and pipers who must be paid pound through my head. But I push them away. After all, if he doesn't return to France, I have nothing to worry about, except for Sergeant Mueller's mad protestations of love. My stomach flip-flops.

"You are not reassured? What's the matter, Marianne?" Stephen asks. "What is it? In a few more days the worst will be over."

Can I confide in Stephen? Will he understand my confusion?

"It's Mueller. He says he loves me," I blurt. "Last night, after Michel left on his mission, Mueller woke before I could go upstairs. He wasn't supposed to. The drug wore off faster than we expected." I cradle Ratcatcher in my arms and bury my head in his soft fur. "I don't understand." I almost choke on the words.

"I do." Stephen smiles a sad smile. "It's the same the world over. Young man meets beautiful girl. You've stolen his heart, m'dear."

"No!" Why does this upset me so?

Ratcatcher leaps onto the small table and crouches like a fluffy white powder puff beside the plate of sausage. "Scram, you bad cat!" I shout, waving my arm at him.

"Leave him be." Stephen strokes Ratcatcher. "I'm not hungry. It's awfully hard to build up any sort of appetite trapped like a mole under the ground."

Ratcatcher licks at a slice of meat with his barbed pink tongue until it is mashed soft enough to eat.

"Mueller's far from home. Lonely. I don't suppose he intended to upset you, Marianne. Your mother says he's not in the least like Bloch."

"*Nobody* is like Bloch," I mutter.

"She insists Mueller is gentle and kind," Stephen continues. "And what's more, he's a talented musician. I like the sound of him."

"But he's an enemy soldier."

"We're all of us swept up in the tides of war. Good people as well as bad. Bloch's the man to fear, m'dear, not our young sergeant."

"Mueller says Bloch has been called back to Germany."

"All the better. Nothing to worry about. But if he returns to this area, stay out of his way. I know his sort. He's up to no good."

★ ★ ★ ★

22

I finish reading Stephen A Tale of Two Cities, and the final words of the novel ring in my ears: *It is a far, far better thing that I do, than I have ever done.* . . . Will I ever manage to do a better thing, I wonder?

Today is warm. Stephen dozes, so I slip away into our humble church of Saint-Gervais. The sweet smell of incense and candle wax mingles with ancient dust and damp stone. Sun filters through the dusty stained-glass windows, spattering the pews with baubles of rainbow light.

I burn candles for Papa and for Stephen and bow to the Holy Mother. My footsteps echo on the flagstone aisle. Plaster saints stare down at me with sad, tormented faces, their garish wounds dripping in hues of oxblood and liver-red. I slide into a pew before the altar, Grand-mère Gruber's rosary beads smooth between my fingers. I raise the silver crucifix to my lips.

I pray for Colonel Bloch to stay in Germany and never return to our town, for Michel to regain his hearing, for Stephen's safe journey to England, and for the end of the war.

I ask God to help me go to art school, to live in Paris, to become a famous designer. Is this selfish? Is

Resistance

God even listening anymore? Probably not. Why should he? The world he created has disappeared in an orgy of fear and hate.

I become aware of strangled coughing at the back of the church. I genuflect before the Holy Mother, then tiptoe down the aisle anxious not to disturb anyone. Many in our congregation stop to pray in these desperate times.

But the hairs on my neck prickle. What can I possibly fear in church? All I see crouched in the back pew is a hunched back. But I smell sawdust. And blood. Not painted blood trickling from the wounds of our plaster saints. Real blood. Of course. It is Philippe Fournier, bound and determined to vex me once again.

"Can't you leave me alone?" I cry. "Especially in church."

He gapes stupidly, clenching the top of the pew in front of him with rough, red hands. Philippe's fingernails are bitten to the quick.

He points toward the altar. "Don't believe a word of it."

"You shouldn't speak this way." I mutter a little prayer under my breath.

"My old man's missing," Philippe croaks.

"Missing? How could he be missing?"

"He's disappeared."

"Where?"

"I don't know."

"You're not making any sense."

"He went out back at noon to slaughter a goat."

Philippe stops talking. I slip into the pew beside him. A damp patch of fresh blood stains the sleeve of his jacket. The smell is sharp and strong. I can scarcely breathe.

"The beast's strung up right enough." Philippe gulps. "The slaughter pen's cleaned, but the old man's vanished."

"Could the Germans have taken him?"

"Not likely."

"But, but he is a—a—"

"A *collaborateur*. Go on. Say it."

"Your papa has hurt a lot of people in this town. He denounced Monsieur Marceau to the Germans for hiding a Jewish child. Maybe someone took revenge."

"Good!" Philippe slams his fist into the wooden pew. "Good riddance to bad rubbish."

"Do you mean that?"

"I don't want him to come home. Ever!"

My skin crawls. I can't imagine feeling this way. "I'm sorry."

"Don't be. I'm not."

"I'll find the priest. You can talk to him. Maybe he—"

But Philippe is already on his feet, pushing past me and barging through the ancient wooden door of the church. The great round iron handle clangs like a giant's gong.

I don't know what to do. I finally decide to follow him into the graveyard. He stands on the path with his shoulders as stiff as a scarecrow's strung across a broomstick. "Let me fetch Father Roulland!" I shout across the ancient toppled gravestones that are cloaked with thick, green moss and worn-away words of love.

"Stay, Marianne."

I hesitate. I so want to leave, but I feel compelled to stay. I don't know why.

"*Your* father's dead!" he shouts.

Resistance

"But I loved my papa," I answer.

Philippe leaps on top of a tomb. The metal studs of his boots clash on the granite surface, echoing eerily around the deserted churchyard. He spins round and round like a crazy man.

"Lucky you, Marianne!" he hollers. "Lucky, lucky you."

Lucky. How can I be lucky? My fingers trace the initials JCL carved so recently on Papa's gravestone. Jean-Claude Labiche. My eyes blur with tears. *Good night, ma chérie, until the day I can return to my dear family, happy and free in our beloved France. . . .*

Dear Papa. You returned to a cold, cold resting place.

★ ★ ★ ★

23

I must pass Fournier's boucherie daily on my way to check M. Bertrand's window. The shop remains shuttered. M. Fournier is not found. Someone has painted COLLABORATEUR in big bold letters across the door, and Philippe does not try to wash the word away.

Tomorrow is August 19, the day planned for Stephen's departure, and we wait anxiously for word that his forged papers will be ready. Time is running out. To my enormous relief I find the bottle in M. Bertrand's window lying on its side, uncorked. I slip inside, and M. Bertrand scribbles the message on a scrap of paper.

Pick up four o'clock

The news fills me with joy. Stephen will be collected tomorrow morning, on schedule, for his train ride to Dieppe. When M. Bertrand is sure I have read the note, he rolls up the paper into a narrow spill and lights his cigar.

"Marianne, before you leave, a word of warning." He lowers himself onto the stool behind the counter.

Familiar spasms of anxiety grip my belly, as M. Bertrand pours a bright pink liquid into a glass bottle. A drop spills onto the countertop and lies there like a cheap, gaudy bead.

"The colonel. Stay well away from him. He's a dangerous man."

"But he's in Germany?"

"As far as we know."

I'm getting tired of all these warnings. I *know* he's dangerous.

"He took advantage of a young girl in Douzlé," adds M. Bertrand, pushing a cork tightly into the neck of the bottle.

"Yes. Jacqueline Duplay. Great-aunt Pauline told Maman about her."

"She's going to have a child," says M. Bertrand.

Ka-boom. My heart thuds in my chest. I can no longer pretend I don't understand the danger I am in. Now it is so obvious. I feel dizzy. If Colonel Bloch tries to rape me, can my little insurance policy save me? Suddenly it all seems extremely unlikely.

"Did Great-uncle Hans receive the package I sent to Köln?" I whisper.

"I believe so, *ma chérie*." M. Bertrand's chubby jowls bounce and bob in distress. "We'll watch out for you, Marianne."

But I refuse to let *anything* spoil today. If the colonel remains in Germany I will be safe, and if Maman heeds Stephen's warning to take no more risks, Michel will be safe too. I *have* to believe that when Stephen begins his journey home, all will be well for us.

It is still dark when we bring Stephen out of the cellar and into the workroom. Maman lights the lamp. Mueller's mound of golden silk sparkles on the table. Not touched since the evening he gave it to me. But not discarded.

"Are you afraid, Stephen?" I whisper.

"Yes," he says gravely. "I can scarcely believe I am

going to see my family again." He grips my hand. "And that you and Michel will finally be safe."

I hope he succeeds. I want him to reach home safely.

"Ready?" Maman hovers behind one of her mannequins.

"Not so loud, Maman. You'll bring the sergeant downstairs."

"Don't fuss. Willi's fast asleep. Besides, he's been avoiding us recently."

Oh, Maman, he's avoiding *me*. It would be obvious to her if she weren't so engrossed in her world of intrigue. Memories of the evening Maman drugged him haunt me. The evening he confessed his feelings for me. And almost kissed me.

"Ta da!" With a flourish she removes the head of the mannequin and delves into the torso, producing a perfect replica of Mueller's uniform.

"Maman, where on earth did you find a hollow dummy?" I gasp.

"It occurred to me after the Germans used their bayonets. Simply pull out the rest of the stuffing and glue the body together again!" She glows with satisfaction and pride.

"My goodness, Emilie dear, you've outdone yourself."

"Yes, I have, haven't I?" She is *so* pleased with herself.

"After the war I will come back to thank you properly. The Labiche family. Henri. Monsieur Bertrand. Bless you all. And what's more, I shall bring my family." Maman tenses, snipping nervously at invisible threads on the uniform. "We'll have the biggest celebration this town has ever seen," Stephen finishes.

He squeezes my hand tightly. "Not only that, m'dear. Marjorie's a doctor. Remember my telling you?"

Resistance

Maman's scissors clatter to the floor. "We'll get that brother of yours to the best specialist we can find, if we have to search the whole world over."

I fling my arms around his neck. "You're the loveliest, nicest, best man we've ever had in our cellar."

"And that's the loveliest, nicest, best compliment I've ever received," he replies.

"Come on. No more nonsense," Maman snaps. "Stephen, get into this quickly. Let's make sure it fits. The courier will be here soon to guide you to the station."

Maman is still fastening the last of the buttons with fidgety fingers when the courier arrives. I don't recognize him. Another anonymous Resistance fighter. To keep us all safe from betrayal.

Betrayal. I'm an expert at the art of betrayal. Not so long ago I almost succeeded in handing over Stephen to the enemy. Stephen, whom I have grown to respect and admire. I stare at him, dressed in the German uniform. A perfect disguise. How happy I am that I failed to betray him.

"Identity papers." The courier is a man of few words. He pulls the forged documents from his jacket.

"Thank you." Stephen slips the papers into his pocket.

"I hope you won't have to use them," Maman frets. "You studied the German textbook I gave you?"

Stephen nods. "If I'm caught in a tight spot, I shall pretend to have laryngitis. With my chest it should be pretty convincing."

He is still wheezy, but Great-aunt Pauline's remedy has worked wonders. That, or the lack of cigarettes.

The escort rocks back and forth on the balls of his feet. "I will ride with you to Caen. Put you on the train

115

to Dieppe." He hands Stephen a rail ticket and a folded newspaper. "When you arrive, wait on the platform. Read this paper until you are approached by our contact. He will say, 'Have a little fishy,' and you will answer, 'On a little dishy,' and he will respond, "When the boat comes in.'"

Stephen nods. "Let's go."

We walk to the back door in a tight huddle. A lump sticks in my throat. I can't swallow.

Maman hugs Stephen first. "Godspeed. I shall miss you, Stephen Crossland." The tic at the corner of her mouth throbs. There's a new sorrow about her I have never seen before. Different from when Papa was lost. Then it was a bitter black anger. Now it is deep despair. Does she truly love this man?

Then me. "Bye," Stephen whispers. "You're a wonderfully gifted girl, Marianne. Lots to live for. *Always* believe that."

And he's gone. Out into the dark morning. Salt air washes in from the sea. From Dieppe.

24

Maman and I creep upstairs to our dark room and lie down on the bed we share, not sleeping, not touching, just staring at the ceiling.

"Stephen will board the milk train to Caen in a few minutes," Maman whispers. "From Caen he will catch the Dieppe express."

"I hope this plan works."

"All we can do now is pray, *ma chérie*. It's in God's hands."

"Why do you care especially about him?"

Maman sighs.

"Please tell me."

"It is so foolish. I involved us in the Resistance to avenge your Papa's death. And then Stephen found his way here. Another soldier from Calais. And suddenly I felt alive again."

Poor Maman. How long would she have gone on pretending he was Papa?

"But we are safe now, aren't we? We no longer need to worry that Mueller will find him in the woodshed?"

"We're safer," Maman murmurs.

"And you will keep your promise to Stephen? You won't involve Michel and me in the Resistance anymore?"

But Maman is sleeping now, curled on her side, snoring softly.

On the roof outside our window a bird chirps, and the first thin streaks of light filter through the curtains. Bit by bit, mottled sunlight dances across the carpet, like cobwebs stretched across hawthorn hedges early in the morning.

Festival day. The German soldiers will be there, just like last year, and the year before. But without the commandant. Such a blessing. His very name sends shivers shuddering down my spine. Stephen sensed he could hurt me. So did Sergeant Mueller. And M. Bertrand, only yesterday. Shall I tell Maman how uneasy I am that he might return one day?

Maman stirs. Stretches. Pours water from the pitcher. Washes swiftly. Slips into her blue crepe.

I sit up in bed, arms around my knees, watching her. "Monsieur Bertrand told me about Jacqueline Duplay. What Colonel Bloch did to her. I'm afraid of him, Maman."

"He's not in France." She pulls back her hair, catching it with a trailing poppy-red scarf. "Even if Bloch returns, he won't accost you in a crowd of people."

Why then, I wonder, did he leave me alone on the deserted château road, when he was free to do what he liked? But I'd kept that part to myself. I could reveal this to Maman now, but I don't.

The wardrobe door is ajar. Something's wrong. What is it? What is missing? I hurtle out of bed and rummage through our sparse collection of shoes, a handbag, and a battered hat box. Papa's briefcase is gone. Vanished. I feel as hollowed out as the mannequin down in the workroom.

"Maman, Papa's briefcase. Where is it?" I lean against the wardrobe for support. "What have you done with it?"

"*Ma chérie*, Papa is gone from us. You must accept that."

Resistance

I know. I do accept it. But never again to hold the old leather bag in my arms? Never to unbuckle it and smell dusty dry textbooks and ink and chalk? Worst of all, my letter is gone. I can't bear it. I slam the door.

"But Maman, there was something in the—"

"Marianne, put on a pretty blouse. Go to the festival. Enjoy yourself. Henri and I will wait in the shop this morning till we get word that Stephen is safely aboard the express to Dieppe."

"Maman, wait—"

"Then we will join you."

"Maman, *please* listen—"

But she's gone, still beset with thoughts of Stephen Crossland and his escape to England.

Later I sit alone on the small stone wall surrounding the fountain in the square and trail my fingers through the cool water. A salty breeze wafts up the river from Cabourg, and a rich smell of fermented apples hangs over the town.

Every year farmers from all over the district set up stalls in the square and offer samples of their home brews, vying fiercely for the accolade of best calvados in Normandy. Despite the presence of German soldiers, there is a genuine holiday atmosphere. Perhaps the absence of commandant Bloch explains the gaiety. A welcome change.

"*Guten Tag*, Marianne."

Boots click. Mueller, of course, a rifle in one hand, clarinet in the other. This is our first encounter since he tried to kiss me. I stare at the cobblestones, avoiding his gaze. Butterflies swoop and swirl in my stomach.

"I am about to inquire whether I may accompany the local band."

"They can hardly refuse you."

The customary flush stains Mueller's cheeks. "Enjoy

yourself today." He bows. I watch him push through the growing throng to reach the bandstand. I wish I had been kinder. I wish I had smiled.

Great-aunt Pauline's café is doing a brisk trade. The tables beneath the awning are filled with soldiers, laughing and joking, but their rifles are stacked ready by the door as usual. It may be a day of celebration, but the Germans are still the conquerors.

Michel staggers about bearing trays laden with food and carafes of wine and cider. I should go and help him, but I want to be alone. Now that Stephen is finally gone from the cellar I cling to the belief Maman will abide by her promise to keep us out of the Resistance. But perhaps Michel will go his own way. He is as obstinate and willful as Maman.

And what of Papa's briefcase containing his letter to me? How could Maman discard it? I will hold the words in my heart till the day I die, but that is not the same as holding them in my hands.

Filled with sadness, I sit by the fountain listening to the music, lulled by the odor of brandy and cheese and barrels of sweet apples. I recall other summers, other festivals, before this horrible war, when Papa was still alive and he and Maman danced and danced around this fountain. Maman always wore a new dress. Curled her hair. Rouged her cheeks. Can Maman really have put Papa right out of her mind so easily?

I am lost in reverie when Philippe appears, pushing through the crowd from the still shuttered *boucherie*. His mob of cronies trails behind, no doubt bent on sharing cigarettes and cider behind the bandstand. Philippe raises his hand. I do the same. Why not? If he doesn't bother Michel, what do I care? They jostle past, hooting and laughing, but Philippe pauses to scoop a handful of water from the fountain. "Leave now!" he mutters. "Hurry!"

"What?" But he's gone. Lost in the crowd.

He's just a fool. An oaf. I try to forget what he said, but my skin tingles. I sense a darkness closing in on me. Why? I try to shake off the feeling of doom. I will go and help Michel in the café until Henri and Maman arrive.

But when I rise, what I see through the flurry and fluster of dancers whirling in time to the music are those familiar legs stretched across the pavement outside the café, bulging out of shining leather boots. He's back! Only the arrogant monster Bloch would insist everyone step around him. Philippe was trying to warn me.

I'm trapped. Bloch's eyes never stray. He snaps a match along the edge of the table and holds the flame to the tip of a cigarette dangling from his lips. He tosses back his head and exhales a plume of smoke. Still he watches. Again he draws deeply. Stares. When there is only a butt left, he mashes it with his heel. Now he boosts himself up from the table and weaves through the crowd. No one sees my plight.

Bloch snatches me from the edge of the fountain. "Time to pay the piper, little beauty," he says, pulling me hard into his chest. The buttons of his jacket scratch my cheeks. "But first, a dance."

He nuzzles his square, pale face into my hair. I can barely breathe. He reeks of tobacco smoke. What's Bloch saying?

"I let you go that day. Remember?" he whispers in my ear. His damp lips nibble my earlobe.

"Don't hurt me," I beg. "I don't know what you mean."

"Don't play games, Marianne." His voice is as cold as his lifeless eyes. His arm is all the way around my waist, pinching and nipping, as he drags me around the square in time to the music. "You weren't alone on the château road."

"Yes, yes I was," I manage to stutter.

"There was someone with you."

"No," I gasp. Thank heaven Stephen is gone from the cellar. Pray God he is well on his way to Dieppe by now.

"Good girls don't tell lies." He twirls me like a whirlwind in furious circles, then the thick bushy fingers grasp my arms.

Oh, dear God, what can I do? Where is Maman? Or Henri? Or Michel? I'm going to faint. The crowd swirls around us. Nobody takes any notice.

"It's time to tell your naughty little secret." Bloch licks his lips like a dog after a bone. Then they are on me, moist and clammy. Pressing hard. I shall be sick. I know I shall. Or worse. My bowels clench and clamp. The foul-tasting, swollen tongue forces my lips apart.

With all my strength I place my hands on his huge, hard chest and push him away. But it's no use. Bloch grabs my blouse, and it rips from shoulder to waist. Buttons shower onto the cobblestones like hail. Can this really be happening? I stare at a livid, red welt on my breast and try desperately to pull the torn blouse across my chest.

"Feisty little thing." Bloch sneers.

When I raise my eyes, what I see is very much worse than the raised mark on my skin.

Michel is careening toward us from the café, a tray piled with dishes high over his head.

"*Non!*" I scream.

"You're not getting away this time." Bloch chuckles, grasping my arm again. "I've waited long enough."

Michel hurls the enormous tray, catching Bloch full in the chest, and down he crashes in a sea of broken glass and spilled drinks.

25

The crowd falls back, utterly silent. No music. No dancing. No laughter. Just a silence settled over the square, thick as a fog on the beach at Cabourg. And Sergeant Mueller is struggling through the throng from the bandstand, his face contorted with rage.

Michel changes course. I lunge, but Michel heads right for Mueller, never breaking stride. Not once. The stride is deliberate. When they draw even, Michel jabs his foot into Mueller's right calf and trips him neatly into a sprawling heap beside the colonel.

"Michel!"

Michel can't hear me. Would he stop if he *could* hear me?

Bloch heaves himself up on his elbow.

"*Halt! Halt!*" The words rattle from his mouth like fire from a machine gun.

But Michel never breaks his even, measured pace. Now he's beyond me, heading out of the square toward the sloping cobbled street leading to school.

Footsteps jangle on the cobblestones behind me. Someone thrusts a jacket into my arms. Shreds of sawdust spatter the sleeves, and an odor of raw meat clings to the fabric, but I don't care. I'm grateful. *So* very grateful. I slip on Philippe's coat and button it across my bare chest.

Now the footsteps scuffle past, catching up with Michel. Philippe and his gang. What do they intend to do? Drag Michel back to Bloch? They circle Michel, dodging and weaving, jeering, teasing. How many times have they taunted Michel? Michel takes no notice, just keeps moving away. So far away.

Bloch is on his feet now, towering over me, his uniform stained with cider and splattered with clumps of soggy bread and soft cheese.

"*Sperren Sie die Stadt!*," screams Bloch, out of control, staggering up and down the cobblestones, kicking at broken glass and dishes.

I know enough German to understand. "Seal off the town." The soldiers at the café and the soldiers scattered around the square jump to attention.

I watch helplessly as Michel continues to walk away. Why, oh why, won't he stop? He's past M. Bertrand's shop now, head erect and shoulders straight. Philippe and his pals continue to worry Michel like a pack of hungry wolves.

Of course. Of course! I know what Philippe is up to. He's protecting Michel. It all makes sense. For two years, Philippe has harassed Michel, but *only* in front of Germans, virtually guaranteeing they would view him as the village idiot. And why? To deflect attention away from Michel's activities in the Resistance! Philippe must be involved too. That's why he referred to Michel as a dummy that day Bloch came to school. I never guessed. Another well-kept secret in my very midst.

"*Tot schiessen! Jeder der sich bewegt!*"

Oh, dear God. "Shoot to kill. Anyone that moves."

In seconds the soldiers grab their rifles, leap into formation, and fan out into the streets surrounding the square.

Philippe hears the order. Of course he does. Bloch's voice is louder than the Cabourg foghorn. The only other sound in the world is the marching boots. Philippe falters. Michel keeps on walking.

I must save my brother. I must. But how? I kneel in the mess of broken glass. "Willi," I plead, "Willi, help me." But he's sprawled on his back in the debris of Michel's tray, dazed. Blood oozes from a cut on his forehead, half hidden under the shock of soft black hair.

"*Tot schiessen!*" bellows Bloch.

I scream.

Philippe and the boys fall back. I can't blame them. Philippe has done all he can. Michel keeps walking.

"Colonel, he's deaf. You know he's deaf." I grab Bloch's shiny black boots. "*Please* don't kill him." I hold on for dear life. I cling to those boots that I so despise, that march, march, march through my head, night and day.

"Somebody's going to pay!" Bloch shouts.

I clutch harder, hugging Bloch's bulging calves, and claw my way up the legs, decorated with blood-red stripes.

"Please, please—"

But it's hopeless. I cannot protect Michel. Bloch wants revenge. A single rifle blast echoes in the narrow street beyond the square. Long before I reach his limp body, I know that I have failed Michel. I have failed Papa. My brother is dead.

★★★★

26

Colonel Bloch wastes no time. I am sitting on a chaise longue in his private office at the château. I recall being in this room once with Maman when she delivered a gown to Countess Yvon. Before the Germans commandeered the château and forced the Yvon family to flee. Before they looted all the artwork and shipped it to Germany. Before they wreaked such havoc on all our lives. A bleak bitterness bubbles inside me. Outside the heavy gilded door the guards march up and down.

I can hardly fathom that Michel is gone from us and that I failed to protect him. I was dragged from his body by soldiers just as Maman and Henri staggered up. Maman cradled Michel's head in her lap and wept. She aged a lifetime today. Her face collapsed, like a piece of crumpled tissue paper, and wrinkles tunneled in around her eyes, nose, and mouth in a matter of moments.

Bloch enters the room wearing a fresh uniform. His cropped red hair is still damp from a bath, and now I am finally alone with the man who is responsible for ordering Michel's death. The man who intends to abuse me in the worst possible way. A black, roiling anger surges through my veins. I can barely control myself. But there is one thing left I must do.

Resistance

"Well, Marianne Labiche. What now?"

Does he expect me to beg for mercy? Never. Never again will I grovel before this monstrous bully. I begged him to spare Michel. I shall *never* in my life beg again. "You wanted to know a secret?" My voice is fierce with loathing. "Well, I'm ready to tell you a secret now."

"I thought you might be." He flings open the French windows, and sweet rose-petal-perfumed air wafts into the room. He stares across the gardens, his great hulking back to me.

The thick oily revulsion drives me on. "Last spring you stole my sketches and sent them to your wife."

"Oh, my little beauty," he murmurs, "we're not here to talk about my wife."

"She wrote to me asking for more designs. I have your address. Gerlach Strasse. Köln."

He suddenly turns from the window and paces across the room, boots grinding into the parquet floor. "Marianne, you are wasting my time."

"I wrote to Frau Bloch about the things you've done to me."

"Done to you!" he bellows. "Nothing yet." He leans over me, his fat, wet tongue darting out of his mouth like a cobra waiting to strike me again. Waves of nausea sweep through my body. What a fool I was to imagine my pathetic insurance policy could work.

"Don't touch me!" I scream.

"Oh, but I shall, little beauty. I shall. I've looked forward to you for a *very* long time." He wrenches Philippe's coat from my shoulders, and his huge paw of a hand reaches for my exposed breast. "Ah, so soft, so—"

"If you hurt me," I gasp, "your wife will receive that letter." I manage to slip beneath his great body and slither across the floor toward the marble fireplace. "My great-uncle Hans lives in Köln," I say, weeping.

Collapsing on the chaise longue, the colonel throws back his head and roars with laughter. "Good God, girl, we're in the middle of a world war. How on earth do you suppose your uncle Hans would know what happens to the likes of you?" He flings his arms above his head. "You think you're so damned important?" He roars with laughter again.

I struggle to keep calm. But the more he laughs at me the angrier I get. Blood pounds through my head, churning like the ocean in a winter gale. I stagger to my feet, clasping my blouse across my breast as best I can.

"The Resistance will know, Colonel. They will make contact immediately. Do you really want to chance that?"

But he's not listening. He leans against the back of the chaise longue, chuckling. "You think my wife cares about a stupid girl making up lies and silly stories?"

"Perhaps not, but she might just care about what you did to Jacqueline Duplay in Douzlé."

"Why, you little bitch!"

"And her condition? Shall I go on?"

Now he's paying attention. He lunges off the price-less couch and kicks it against the wall. One delicate gilt leg splinters. He advances toward me very, very slowly. He will rape me now. Then kill me. I am sure of it.

On the mantelpiece is a silver frame. Two girls with masses of red, curling hair gaze down at me. I grab the photograph and hurl it at Colonel Bloch as hard as I can. "Go ahead. Hurt me. *Nothing* you can do to me can be worse than murdering Michel!" I scream, staring into his cruel, gray eyes. "Do you really want Ingrid and Erika to find out that their father rapes young girls? Do you?"

Miraculously he stops. His face flames a red as rich

as port wine. The huge, ugly hands with thick, hairy fingers dangle loose by his sides. For the longest time we just stare at each other.

"Do you have any idea where I've been?" He grunts. The booming voice has gone. He's deflated, like a punctured balloon. "No, of course you don't."

He falls to his knees and grovels through the broken glass, trying to retrieve the picture of his daughters from the shattered frame. He stabs at the photograph, cutting his finger on a jagged piece of glass. "Ingrid and Erika are dead."

"What?" I gasp. Is God so ruthless? What did they ever do to deserve death?

"The British bombed Köln in May." Saliva gathers at the corner of Bloch's mouth. "An unexploded bomb somehow lodged beneath our garden wall, and there it remained for two months."

The colonel struggles to his feet. Glass crunches under his boots. His eyes are bloodshot. Mucous drips from his nose.

"Then one day, walking home from school, my girls triggered the bomb. It blew them to kingdom come."

He finally succeeds in pulling the photograph free of the frame, but drops of blood smudge the print.

"They killed my girls," he screams. Holding the picture close to his face, he contemplates the blood-stained images of Ingrid and Erika.

"*You* killed my brother." And now, at last, I am finished. I have absolutely nothing more to say.

The photograph slips from Bloch's fist, and the hairy fingers struggle with the holster strapped to his belt. I am to die. Just like Michel. So let it be now. I drag myself across the room through shards of glass, past

Bloch's desk, to the open window. The scented breeze soothes the stinging wound on my breast. I wait for the bullet to pierce my back. Like the bullet that took Michel's life.

Click. Click. Inexplicably the gun clatters onto the floor behind me. Bloch moans. An anguished, agonized cry of despair. He lurches across the room to the French window and clutches at the sweeping tapestry curtains. His stale breath blows across the back of my neck. Somehow I find the strength to step out onto the terrace and stagger through the rosebeds.

"Get out of my sight!" Bloch bellows. "Go!"

27

I rest in Papa's rocking chair, and Maman bathes my cut in a mixture of water and calvados. I have won. Bloch won't touch me now, but it's a hollow victory. So hollow.

"Marianne, *ma chérie*, speak to me," Maman begs. I hear her voice, but she sounds far, far away. At last, mercifully, I feel nothing. Nothing at all.

"Did he hurt you more?" Tears pour down Maman's cheeks as she eases my arms into a fresh blouse. "Did he touch you, did he . . . ?"

She can't even say the word. Rape. Ratcatcher curls into my stomach and purrs. I manage to shake my head no. I can't speak. There's nothing more to be said.

Maman kneels on the hearthrug beside me. Blood stains her blue crepe dress. Michel's blood. Dear Michel. Gone forever. I could only protect myself.

"Say something to me. Anything." Maman's skin is waxy, like the face of an old dolly. She chafes my cold hands between her own quivering fingers. But I can't. The most terrible thing in the world has happened. Michel is dead. Dead. Dead. Dead. Because he took one last great risk. For me. He valued my life above his own.

Footsteps pound up the stairs. Willi. He taps on the parlor door before entering. A bloody bandage swathes his head, and his uniform stinks of sour wine, rotting food.

"Madame Labiche. I'm so sorry. Michel was—"

"Bastard!" Maman's face contorts with fury. "You *Boche* are all the same—"

"I'm truly sorry."

"Brute. Get out of my house."

Willi turns to me. Kneels down, grasps my hand.

"Marianne, *Liebchen*, are you all right? Listen, please. I did not want any of this to happen. I tried to stop Bloch."

"Don't touch her!" Maman screams, wrenching his hand away.

Willi rises slowly and looks Maman right in the eye. "Believe me, Madame, I am not a monster. I did not report the fugitive in your woodshed."

"You knew?" Maman gasps.

"*Ja.* I knew." Willi shrugs. "Now I must change my uniform. Report back to the château. The Allies attempted a futile invasion today at Dieppe—"

"Dieppe?" Maman clutches her belly. "You said Dieppe?" She howls, raw and primitive, like an animal caught in a trap.

"*Mein Gott.*" Willi stares at her. "You have tried to move the Englishman?" He grabs Maman's arms and shakes her hard. "Through Dieppe?" He shakes her again. "Tell me!"

Maman stares back at Willi, trying to compose herself, but the tic at the side of her mouth twitches furiously. Willi's no fool. He'll figure it out.

He crouches again beside the rocking chair. "Marianne, nothing will ever change the way I feel about you. Give me a word of hope? Please? Before I go."

Resistance

But I can't. I struggle past him to the back window with Ratcatcher in my arms. I rub my cheek against his warm fur, and his purrs rumble through my cold body.

I gaze over the backyard, the empty cellar beneath the woodshed, across the rooftops to the woods where Michel picked up Stephen last spring, and the other way toward the sea, to Dieppe.

Willi's behind me. So close I hear his heart beating. "Marianne." His voice cracks. "I love you," he whispers. "I will help you. *Just* tell me I have a chance with you."

I turn away from the window. A bright red flush suffuses his face. His eyes glisten. I try to speak, but my throat is closed tight. It's useless. I can't say a word. I know the words Willi wants to hear, but they are lodged so deep inside me I can't reach them.

Willi spins around, his heels click, and he leaves the house.

★★★★

28

"Willi will certainly turn us in now," says Maman, from Papa's rocking chair, defeated at last. "Who can blame him? I don't understand why he kept our secret in the first place." She shakes her head. "But he must surely protect himself now, before it's too late."

She gets up and goes downstairs to unlock the shop door. So the Germans won't have to break it down, I suppose, when they come to arrest us. Poor Stephen, out in the open, masquerading as a German sergeant. How long can he possibly survive? Normandy will be swarming with German troops in response to the failed Allied attack at Dieppe. Will there ever be a successful attack? Or will we live in terror forever?

Maman wraps a shawl around my shoulders and helps me back into the rocking chair. "I'll make us some tea." Ratcatcher purrs and sighs as I settle him again into my lap. I smooth his silky white fur. Maman and I wait in the parlor all night long. Once in a while I try to move my lips, clear my throat, but I can't.

Far away, guns boom along the coast. Once, on rue Saint-Gervais, a patrol marches past, not coming for us. Not yet. The clock in the church tower chimes each long, unbearable hour of our ordeal.

Resistance

"If I had listened to you, Marianne, we would not have lost Michel." Now it is Maman who is weeping. "I was so overwhelmed with bitterness when your papa died, I couldn't see what I was doing." In the lamplight her cheeks shimmer with tears. "Papa would never have allowed me to involve children in the Resistance. Especially not you and Michel."

I stroke her hand a little to let her know I hear.

"But why did Michel do it? Draw attention to himself like that? I don't understand, Marianne."

No, she doesn't. She overlooked so much. Bloch's cruelty. Willi's love for me. Michel's determination to make his own choices. And his foolish idea that my life and Willi's were worth more than his own. What a burden to bear. To live with for the rest of my life. I rest my head, which is numb with pain, on Maman's shoulder. Finally, motorbike tires screech to a stop on the cobblestones outside the shop.

"They're here now, Marianne. Be brave." We stand, hand in hand, beside the fireplace. "It will soon be over," Maman whispers. "All over."

A German voice shouts outside, then we hear a thump and bump like a sack of potatoes being dragged up the stairs. I hold Maman's hand tight. My heart hammers in my chest so hard I think I'll explode. I smell brandy, even before the parlor door opens. Dear God, drunk, too. I'll be all right if they don't torture us first. I don't want to be tortured. My eyes fill with tears. A boot thuds against the door, and it bursts open. Ratcatcher streaks beneath the dresser.

But it isn't armed soldiers. It's Willi, his uniform drenched with brandy, holding up another German soldier who is either very drunk or very ill. I stare past Willi, expecting the firing squad to be right behind him.

"What a night, eh, Otto?" shouts Willi. "Best brandy in the world."

He shoves Otto into the rocking chair. "Sleep it off, old friend. Too much of a good thing!"

"How dare you, Willi? Get your drunken friend out of my house!" Maman splutters in rage.

Willi places his fingers on his lips. "Get rid of the German uniform, papers, quick!" he urges.

"Stop playing stupid games," Maman shouts. "I'm sick of you bastards. Arrest us, and get it over with."

Otto coughs. A familiar, wracking cough. Maman stiffens. She releases my hand, and bending over, removes his cap. "Stephen!" Maman gathers him in her arms and plants whispery little kisses all over his face and hands.

Somehow, Willi has managed to return Stephen to us. He shouts again. "What you need is a good rest, Otto. Overdid it just a bit, eh?" He mutters in Maman's ear, "Sorry, but it is necessary, in case we were followed."

Maman finally understands. "But Willi," she stammers, "where did you find him?" She drags herself away from Stephen's slumped body. "How did you know where to look?"

"I guessed. When the invasion began, all the trains to Dieppe were canceled and returned to their original departure points," Willi explains in a low voice. "I found him hiding in the latrines at the train depot in Caen. I pretended he was a buddy on leave, much the worse for wear. I splashed us both with a bottle of brandy before bringing him back on the motorbike."

"But why didn't you just turn him in? I don't understand."

"Marianne understands."

Yes, I do. I truly understand. Willi risked court martial for my sake. He truly loves me. Tears fill my eyes.

Resistance

"Just trust me, Madame," Willi says. "Hide him again. And may God give you *all* the strength to survive."

We *must*. For Michel's sake. It's what he died for.

Maman sinks to her knees again beside the rocking chair and cradles Stephen in her arms as though her very life depends on it. Perhaps it does. Yes, I see now that it most certainly does.

"Come." Willi takes my elbow and guides me downstairs to Maman's workshop. He throws open the shutters. A ruby-red sun is rising over the chimney pots and rooftops. Ribbons of vivid mauve cloud stream across the sky.

In a dim, dark corner of the room I spy a bulging canvas kit bag, a clarinet case, and a bundle of sheet music. So I am to lose Willi, too.

He strokes my hair. "I have orders to the Russian front."

Willi clasps my hand. His palm feels cool, smooth, like a pebble from the river Dives. Like one of Michel's pebbles.

"I will cherish you for all time," Willi whispers.

He is bathed in the plummy morning light filtering through the window. I am hypnotized by the crimson glow and raise my hand to trace the outline of his face. Slowly my fingertips memorize Willi's eyebrows, the imposing nose, high cheekbones, full lips, and jutting chin. All this I fix in my heart, along with the words of Papa's letter and Michel's great courage. Memories.

Willi's silk still lies abandoned on Maman's worktable. He gathers up the fabric and wraps it about my shoulders. "Marianne, make a wondrous creation. Then no matter what happens, I can imagine my beloved girl draped in golden silk." Tears spill down his cheeks. "Will you do this for me?"

"Yes, Willi," I whisper. "I will do it for both of us."

I cling to him. And I kiss his lips. Honeysuckle sweet. Another memory to treasure. After endless moments, I watch Willi cross the workroom and gather up his belongings. And I know in my soul that Willi is disappearing from my life forever.

The silk slips from my shoulders. I smooth it gently onto the cutting table. It is cool as glass beneath my fingers. Shadows gleam in the peach-blush light.

I *shall* create a truly wondrous *robe de chambre* with Willi's glittering cloth. With every stitch I will sew a seed of hope. Hope for us all.

Epilogue

TWO YEARS LATER, ON JUNE 6, 1944, AMERICAN,
BRITISH, AND COMMONWEALTH TROOPS LAUNCHED A
SUCCESSFUL INVASION ALONG THE NORMANDY COAST,
WHICH FINALLY FREED THE FRENCH PEOPLE FROM
GERMAN OPPRESSION.